# FAMILY MATTERS

LIES ACROSS TEXAS

A BLACK ORCHID ENTERPRISES MYSTERY
BOOK 3

M. R. DIMOND

## Content Warning

This book is intended for an adult audience, and may contain language, characters, themes, and content that are offensive or triggering to some readers.

# CONTENTS

# TRAVELS WITH THE BLACK ORCHIDS

# CHAPTER 1
# JD THOMPSON: THURSDAY, BEAUCHAMP, TEXAS

I love early morning office sounds: the four Very Good Kitties scrabbling down the dark-wood gallery floor, my partner Dianne Cortez doing syncopated samba steps on the way to her office in one of the first-floor turrets, a cat yowling in my other partner Johnny Ly's vet clinic, and at our reception desk, our intern Darryl Swann practicing the soprano part to "Dancing Queen" in Spanish. Just a normal August morning in your normal detective's office in disguise as a law, accountancy, and veterinary firm—and an ABBA tribute band.

I admit that's not how it was either in the judge's chambers or the corporate law firm where I used to work. I left them behind in Austin, Texas, when I fled with my friends to the nearby tiny town of Beauchamp. Now we work and live in Gregg House, an old Victorian mansion whose date plaque reads 1897. No doubt the house has seen many things in its hundred-plus years, but I still imagine its two ornate turret roofs as eyebrows raised in surprise at its latest denizens.

August in Texas makes me think of Paris. Not that it reminds me of Paris—au contraire, mes amis. But as I swelter and sweat in Beauchamp, I remember those glorious four months after college, before law school, when I wandered the banks of the Seine and wrote poetry in sidewalk cafés on breezy, warm days. Parisians complained about their weather, but only because they'd never been to Texas. I considered every day perfect, and when Dianne, then a different kind of partner, joined me in August, every day doubled in perfection. As the numbers maven, she said that was impossible, but I know better.

The phone shrilled, interrupting my remembrance of things past and kicking me back into my office in Gregg House's other turret.

Darryl answered in a completely different voice, "Black Orchid Enterprises. Law offices of James Daniel Thompson. May I help—Just a moment. I'll see if Mr. Thompson is available."

He tiptoed into my office and mouthed, "JD, it's your father."

I made a gagging face and picked up the phone. "Hi, Dad. Got just a few minutes between clients—" If you define *a few* as those between 9:30 a.m. and 2:00 p.m.

"I won't keep you," he snapped. "When's the last time you heard from Merry?"

I frowned, thinking. At age twenty, my twin sisters would soon enter their last year of college in Waco, where Dad's parents lived. Merry and Cherry didn't have keeping in touch with their brother high on their to-do list. "Not sure. I usually see them when I visit the grandparents, when we get everybody together for a meal. But Merry went to Dallas for the summer, and—"

"I'm not sure she did. I tried to call her when I was in Dallas last week. I stopped by the place she said she worked too. She hasn't been there in months."

Idly I wondered if he would ever let me finish a thought or a sentence. I remembered Merry's social media post about getting a job at Doo Wop Burger, one of those trying-to-be-vintage diner chains. She was wearing their terminally cute uniform and posing with a silly grin in front of their icon, a huge dancing cheeseburger.

Dad growled, "Your grandparents haven't seen her recently. She or Cherry came home to Houston every other weekend this summer, always wanting money. But Merry never said she'd left that job, and she never sent me her Dallas address."

I heard a sliver of worry in his voice. Touching, it was. "I'll check with Dianne. The twins still stay in touch with her. Cherry doesn't know anything either?"

"She says not. She says she and Merry have been trying to live their own lives instead of being practically Siamese twins. They planned to live separately this summer, with Merry going to Dallas to pursue some guy." The disapproval faucet was on full blast.

I remembered Merry's Instagram photo with the caption "Going to Dallas to be near my darling J!"

My father's cough summoned me back to the present. "They've exchanged texts over the summer, nothing that alarmed Cherry. She's sure Merry will show up before the semester starts."

"I'm sure she's right," I agreed, based on nothing at all. "I'll ask around and get back—well, goodbye and you have a nice day too," I said to the dial tone.

A note from Darryl popped up in our interoffice chat app, proving that he could work and sing at the same time: his suggestions for the next week's social media. Besides answering the phone, Darryl helps with my routine legal forms and Dianne's routine tax forms, assists Johnny in the cat clinic and shelter, and handles our social media. He even has a blog on our website he calls Swann's Way.

I can't see the point in advertising Black Orchid Enterprises to the world when we're geographically confined to Central Texas, just south of Austin, but I'm told you never turn down free advertising. Who knows when someone nearby might be looking for an accountant, lawyer, or vet, or maybe all three?

Darryl also handles office holiday decorations, which have landed us on TV, not always in a positive way. I couldn't think of any holidays in the near future, so I thought we were safe for a while. I couldn't say that often, considering how many cultures we represent, a regular United Nations of an office: Standard White Guy (me), Mexican (Dianne), Vietnamese (Johnny), Jewish (Johnny), and Black (Darryl and Chantal Gaumont, accountant, soprano, and leader of our band). Even then, sometimes he'll find some other holiday that he only partially understands.

Being the bosses, we could shut him down, but holiday decorating and social media are his favorite duties, and we're not that far away from our own trash jobs to want to take that joy from him. Also, his efforts bring more people into the office.

For Throwback Thursday, Darryl proposed a Thompson family

Easter photo from around fifteen years ago: Young Teen Me, forcing up the corners of my mouth despite clenched teeth, my hands clawing the shoulders of two wiggly twins, already sugared up on their Easter candy breakfast, their ruffly blue spring dresses matching their skin, because Texas always turns arctic for Easter just to show that it can.

After all those years, I could still hear the conversation. Dad complaining: "Adrienne, we're going to be late for church." Mother, frustrated but determined: "I still don't have a good picture of them in their dresses. JD, would you hold them still?" That was the twins' cue to ramp it up to eleven. It was an Easter miracle that we were all in focus. I've always known that the answer to the Biblical question "Am I my sisters' keeper?" was "You better believe it."

I hesitated to approve the photo but couldn't think of a reason to object. We had already posted Dianne at age five, dancing the Macarena at one of her mother's parties, and eight-year-old Johnny helping in his grandfather's Vietnamese restaurant in downtown Beauchamp. It was my turn, and if I rejected this one, the next suggestion would be worse, maybe the last Easter photo before Mother died, when we all knew what was coming. The twins had grinned like maniacs over their holiday ruffles, and I didn't look any better.

Nobody smiled in the following year's photo, with Cherry as Goth as a twelve-year-old was allowed to be and Merry in a colorless straight shift, her hair bobbed into a straight line that echoed her compressed lips. I looked like I had a toothache while still auditioning for Future Lawyers of America. Dad didn't bother with Easter photos after that.

The twins had a lifelong history of cute. Mother adored her blonde, curly-haired, blue-eyed twins. After inflicting old-fashioned family names on them (Meredith Arline and Charity Adrienne), she nick-named them Merry and Cherry, making a case for naming kids later, after you know them. Merry is more thoughtful than giggly, and Cherry isn't generous. From the day they were born, shortly before my ninth birthday, Mother dressed them in pastels, with maximum ribbons, ruffles, and bows. They looked like frilly potatoes, despite being skinny as pencils.

I admit I was underwhelmed to receive two baby sisters instead of a

PlayStation. And even with just a vague concept of where babies came from, I was nauseated.

I spent my teen years babysitting them, which didn't improve our relationship. After our mother died of cancer when they were eleven and I was nineteen, I made a point of going home more, the better for us to be miserable together. I also brought them to visit me at college, where I lived with ten or so housemates, all female except for Johnny, in a rickety old mansion we named Casa Cortez, because Dianne (of course) had organized us into it. Hanging out with the big girls filled the twins with pride; they ignored me. I thought when they themselves entered college we might have adult friendships, but they didn't have much use for an older brother unless they needed help moving.

I tapped a brief text to Merry before walking across the hall. It's more of a gallery, extending from the front to the back of the house, wide enough to be a room in its own right. Darryl had moved on to "Chiquitita." As I passed the reception desk, I sang a few notes of my bass-baritone part, just for encouragement.

Sometimes Dianne's mother, an event planner, booked MultiABBA for one of her parties when Chantal had another gig as a soloist. She's the only one of us who can claim to be a full-time musician, except for when she helps us during tax season. Darryl hoped to substitute for Chantal when she was unavailable.

When I walked into Dianne's office, she was gazing at her monitor with a rapt expression that meant either (1) she was in love or (2) she'd just created the most awesome spreadsheet ever. I was going with the latter. Her deep, happy sigh meant that she'd beaten the numbers into submission yet again. Nevada, her golden-pointed, blue-eyed Siamese cat, slept on her desk, within easy petting range.

I always thought Dianne the most gorgeous woman I'd ever seen, even as my three-time ex: almost six feet of warm brown skin and blacker-than-black hair shining around her shoulders in thick waves. As I fiddled with my phone, I asked, "Dianne, have you heard from Merry?"

"No, I heard from Cherry recently though." Being Dianne, she then proceeded to check her answer by scrolling through past texts. She frowned. "I'm wrong. Merry texted me about three weeks ago. Nothing much, just checking in. But Cherry did text me a few days before that, asking whether I thought she should change her name to Cheryl or Cherie. She's worried that no one will take her seriously as Cherry, except maybe in adult films. I must have been thinking of that."

My sisters met Dianne when they were ten, when I brought Dianne home for some holiday as The Girlfriend™. After we broke up for the first time less than a year later, they sobbed to Dianne, "But you don't have to break up with *us*." Dianne agreed and took them under her wing because, as she said, "What's two more in my family group?"

The eldest of five siblings and many, many cousins, Dianne will tell you in the first ten minutes on your first date that she's never having children. That never stopped her from taking her sisters and cousins at least twice a year to buy clothes. Her mother and aunts were confident that she'd choose things for modest Catholic girls, and the girls were sure that she would make all their fantasies of style and allure come true. It was a testament to Dianne's skills that all parties always thought they got what they wanted.

Merry and Cherry were thrilled to join the Cortez pilgrimages to the Hillsboro discount mall. A few years after our mother died, Grandmother made the ceremonial trip to a Houston Merle Norman store so they could learn about makeup, but, not laboring under the same delusions as the Cortez mothers, she was glad to have Dianne's help with fashionable clothes and later, a trip to Planned Parenthood for all the essentials of young womanhood. Merry and Cherry made fast friends with Dianne's sisters closest to their own ages, Tima and Juke. The Cortez brother, Zap, two years older, grew more admiring as the twins matured and sometimes claimed that he needed to go on the shopping trips too.

Guadalupe Dianne Cortez and her siblings were a testament to their mother's devotion to the Virgin Mary. Instead of naming them all María, Conchita Cortez chose names of Marian shrines, with backup Anglo names for emergencies. Dianne claimed her middle name in college after a lifetime of schoolyard teasing about "Lupita." So I could see why Cherry would turn to her for advice. Our mother loved Cherry's nickname, but there were limits to what a girl could do for her dead mother. Cherry worked it as best she could, often wearing cherry-colored clothes, dying her hair cherry red, and collecting cherry blossom jewelry and fascinators.

My phone dinged a notification in response to my earlier text. I shrugged at the results. "Merry's got auto-respond on for texts, probably voice too."

> Can't answer my phone at work. Back atcha later.

"Problem?" asked Dianne as she stroked Nevada's forehead.

I leaned against the dark-wood door jamb. "My father's worried about Merry. He visited the place she was supposed to be working in Dallas and found she hadn't been in for months. So he—and I—are looking for people who've heard from her recently."

Dianne's eyebrows rose in wonder. She said in a hushed voice, "Wow. Your father called you for help." She focused on her screens and typed a bit before saying, "I just sent a blast to all my sisters and cousins, asking for the last time anyone heard from her. Merry and Cherry are on my hermanas y primas list too; maybe they'll realize people are worried."

Footsteps in the hall announced the approach of Dr. John Ky Ly, our other partner, after his morning vet appointments. "JD, would you come with me on a justice of the peace call? We can bring back lunch."

I jumped as I conflated his actions with my own worries. As assistant justice of the peace, Johnny had to examine every dead body in Alvarez County. But Merry lived in Waco. Maybe Dallas. She couldn't be the dead body he was going to see. Definitely probably not.

# CHAPTER 2
# JD: THURSDAY, RURAL ALVAREZ COUNTY

Texas elects justices of the peace to preside over small claims court, perform weddings, and pronounce people dead. JPs also help determine the need for further investigation into the death. Kevin Dixon, the elected justice of the peace, was the owner-manager of the local Sonic Drive-In. Though he'd studied hard to perform the first two responsibilities, he was happy to hire Johnny to do the third. As a vet, Johnny had more experience with corpses than Kevin got in his two-week training.

Dianne made a face. "You're going to bring lunch after you've had your hands on a dead body?"

I agreed. "That's as bad as when he wanted to fix dinner after substituting for one of the country vets and spent the afternoon shoving his arm up seventy-five cow butts."

Dianne frowned, and I realized I had said the wrong line. She had started the complaint, so I was supposed to be the soother. But I wanted to complain.

"I always wear gloves. I wash and scrub my hands too," protested Johnny. "Are you coming with me, JD?"

Dianne shook her head and turned back to her screens.

I made an effort not to sigh. Johnny can provide the necessary information to law enforcement and the county attorney: Is the person dead?

Naturally? Does any evidence warrant further investigation? But he relies on me as his interpreter—excuse me, legal counsel—with the rest of the world. Since he thinks more deaths should be investigated than law enforcement does, he likes having me along as a buffer, at least when we're dealing with the sheriff's office. Local police he can handle; most of them come to his community meals on Friday nights.

I replied, "Sure. If you drive. I need to reach Cherry."

Riding in his F-100, bought used from a rancher who had bounced it over bumpy fields for many years, was a sacrifice. If he'd asked me, I'd have suggested buying a truck built after he was born. The original two-toned reds had long ago faded to a single grayish pink in the broiling Texas sun. Johnny, like our neighboring farmers and ranchers, needed a working truck, not a modern behemoth with every luxury feature except a mint on the pillow at night. Our neighbors took care of their trucks so they would run for decades, Johnny claimed.

That care extended only to the motors. The standard cab interior appeared to have been decorated by a badger. A blanket lay over the bench seat to help smooth out the lumps of dribbling stuffing. The badger might have replaced the passenger seat belt too. Retraction happened in slo-mo, usually after something hit the windshield or ceiling. Johnny had ordered a new seat and seat belts, but parts that old are hard to find. In the meantime, he drives below the speed limit as he tries to avoid the worst parts of the obstacle courses Texas calls roads.

Our destination, a ranch on the far edge of Alvarez County, was around twenty minutes away, twenty minutes of banging my head on the ceiling as we bounced down rural roads. But I needed to call Cherry.

"Really?" she demanded as a greeting. "First Dad, then Dianne and her whole family. Now you."

"Great to talk to you too. Where's Merry?"

"At her stupid job, I guess. That's what her phone says. Why does everybody want to know all of a sudden? I do have a job, you know."

With a murmured apology, Johnny launched over a deep, unavoidable gash in the country road. I winced as my head smacked the side window. "I'm sure the Waco Arts Association can spare their intern a minute to soothe her family's worries."

What Cherry really wants to do is act, but she's majoring in arts management in hopes of having a salary until fame and fortune find her.

She made a sound, sort of a laugh and snort. "Dad? Worried?"

"In his own way, sure. I'm concerned in *my* own way that she doesn't seem to be at the job she started early in the summer."

"She probably got another one and just didn't say. With restaurants, who cares?"

I saw the next rut in time to hunch down. "Who's J?"

"Huh?"

"The J she went to Dallas to be near."

"Some guy she met in her classes. I didn't know him. She wasn't sure it was going anywhere, so she didn't make a big deal about it."

"Just moved to Dallas to be near him. What's his name?"

"Dunno. Jason, Julian, Juan, Jamal, something."

"Well, we hope to meet him soon. And Dad won't be concerned if he knows one of us talked to her recently. Have you, in the last day or so?"

"We mostly text. I'm sure she sent me something recently. This was supposed to be her summer of independence, remember?"

"Have you two fallen out?"

"With my twin? God, JD. How is that even possible? It's just, we've lived together all our lives, from conception. I'm so glad, because when Mommy died, what if I didn't have a twin? I'd be like you. And I will be, after graduation. Then she'll go somewhere to play in the mud, and I'll go to some big city. So we thought we should try living alone for the summer to get ready for that day. Well, Merry did."

"That's Merry, always planning ahead."

"Yeah, that's why she's graduating early next December and I'm graduating in May. And she's taking a bunch of stupid gimme-A courses that everybody else took three years ago, while she jumped right into math and science, and she went to summer school every year, and now she's going to coast through her last semester and focus on getting a job or applying to grad school. But I'm not bitter."

Merry was getting some kind of environmental science degree, focusing on water and marine life, judging from eye-glazing conversations at holiday dinners.

I applied some butter. It couldn't hurt. "You spent your summers in theater productions, focusing on your career in a different way. You'll both do great, I'm sure."

"Yeah, maybe we and our friends will go to some hick town, and I'll start a little theater group, and Merry can direct the ecology of the stock ponds."

Like her brother and his college roommates? I refused to rise to the Cherry-bait and said, "We all have our own definitions of success. Tell Merry to call me so we'll leave you alone." Appealing to Miss Charity's self-interest usually worked better than asking her to be considerate.

She said something I chose to believe was a farewell and hung up.

"Any data?" asked Johnny, as though he couldn't have figured out the other side of the conversation.

"It doesn't rise to the level of data or court-room evidence," I said. "Hearsay and calls for speculation on the part of the witness, which are fine for everyday life. And Cherry's annoyed enough to track down her sister and make her call somebody."

I don't know if twins really are telepathic, but I felt better knowing that Cherry wasn't worried. She's the sharp-edged twin, both in looks and personality. Her style, once freed of Mother's influence, was all angles, from her straightened hair, cut in triangles, to her unadorned outfits with geometric patterns, all neutral tones, except for the occasional splash of (you guessed it) cherry. Embracing a softer look, Merry let her hair curl around her shoulders and occasionally gave in to a few furbelows that Mother would have liked, if only there were more of them.

Johnny asked, "What was her definition of success?"

"Cherry said she'd start a little theater in some hick town and Merry could play in the local stock ponds. Snarking against Black Orchid Enterprises, you know," I explained.

Johnny shrugged. "I like our arrangement."

The sign in front of Gregg House reads:

BLACK ORCHID ENTERPRISES
G DIANNE CORTEZ, CPA, CFE

## Dr. John Ky Ly, DVM, Veterinary Acupuncture, Practice Limited to Cats
## JD Thompson, Attorney and Mediator

Our diversity cred spans the bottom of the sign: Se Habla Español Aquí followed by something illegible that Johnny said meant the same thing in Vietnamese.

We have not always lived in the castle, but when Johnny's grandmother wanted to move to an assisted living complex, she asked Johnny if he wanted to take over Gregg House, her behemoth home plopped in the middle of Beauchamp (pronounced Beecham), Texas, just outside Austin. Johnny, recovering at an ashram after burning out in his zoo vet residency, set up a new life that he could handle, which included a part-time vet practice and inviting two of his college roommates to move in. Dianne and I gave our families whiplash as we swerved off our individual highways to success and set up our offices in the turrets that guarded Gregg House. They, with Johnny's clinic at the back of the house, draw a fine metaphor for our relationship.

Gregg House and its land are big enough to hold all the houses on the surrounding blocks. The house itself has enough space for our offices and the clinic downstairs and living space upstairs. Outside there's a garden, a cat environment adapted from a barn-like garage (currently holding thirteen cats that Animal Control picked up), Johnny's meditation room (formerly his grandfather's), and a row of several small apartments, one of them Darryl's home.

I'm happy with the office and living arrangements, even when I accompany Johnny on his justice of the peace outings. I thought it would be too depressing for him, looking at dead bodies, but I'm the one that keeps a distance from the corpse. I'm just there to provide legal muscle, or the appearance of it, but I can do that without the close examination Johnny does. He says he views it as a last honor he can give a once-living soul. I'm not sure if that's from his Jewish or his Buddhist philosophy.

As Johnny pulled on the hazmat suit that would let him get close to the body, I surveyed the situation. Did the entire shift of the sheriff's office turn out? Many uniformed folks stood around the scene of the crime, a clearing on the deserted ranch, under a pecan tree. Mesquite, tall grasses, and rattlesnakes had taken over the rest of the ranch.

As a precautionary defense against crime scene odors, I held my breath as I followed Johnny. I kept my eyes on the ground, though I'd be more likely to hear the rattle before seeing a snake. Snakes get mad in the hot summer months.

I nodded to each one of the officers. The size of their contingent indicated a serious, complicated crime. But their smirks didn't match that conclusion. I allowed a bit of air in my nostrils, enough to confirm the lack of coppery blood and pungent organics of standard violent death scenes. Johnny's face showed nothing, like usual, and he pulled out his super-duper crime scene camera and clicked away as he inched in a wide arc around the area.

Now the officers were grinning. An occasional guffaw escaped. Johnny moved in closer. I always use my lack of crime scene booties and hazmat suit as an excuse to keep back. But now I let my eyes follow Johnny as he knelt on the ground. He snapped a few more photos before bringing out his lab kit. I coughed to disguise a snort of laughter.

The deputies exchanged amused glances as the sheriff took control of the situation. "Son, I know you're just a vet, but you do realize that's not a body?"

"It looks like a Princess Leia sex doll, D cup model. Or used to be. I'll confirm that," said Johnny as he worked, taking samples of this and that. "I appreciate your calling me out. It gives me a chance to fully work a crime scene without getting in your way. JD, can you get me a leaf bag from the truck? It will make a good body bag."

I chuckled silently as I did. When I returned, Johnny was setting out crime scene flags to mark possible clues in the area. No one was smiling now.

Sheriff Dane growled in the voice that made most people think twice about what they were doing, "*Why* do you think you're taking the, um, body?"

Johnny, being socially clueless, replied before resuming with the camera. "So I can perform my own lab tests and gather DNA."

One of the younger deputies shifted position, like mesquite thorns were sticking through his boots. "You're having DNA analyzed?"

"Certainly I am. There's no harm in it, and it gives me a chance to interpret the results."

"But then somebody's DNA is in a database without their permission," argued the sheriff.

"No one asks criminals if they want their DNA in a database," Johnny replied.

"There's no crime committed, and the county's not paying for a worthless test!"

"Of course not. I'll pay for my own training, and there are places that will run DNA for free." Johnny had been ducking and darting about in a screwball Dance of the Evidence, but now he stood straight and looked up into the sheriff's eyes. "The crime at a minimum is littering."

I approached the torn, deflated plastic body with the bag. "No law against picking up litter."

"I hope to determine whether the destruction happened naturally, as a result of the elements, or whether someone intentionally inflicted the damage on his toy. I'll send you a report on my findings. Frankly, I would be concerned about someone who plays at murder."

That shut them up. I studied their expressions as I held the bag open for Johnny to deposit the deceased doll. One of my old piano pieces, "Pavane for a Dead Princess" played in my mind. The somber expressions around me were now more in keeping with that music and the occasion, and more than one person looked concerned.

I placed Leia, fantasy of my young teen years, gently in the back of the cab while Johnny collected his evidence—cigarette butts, a beer can, and other detritus. I hoped he wouldn't want to hold a funeral after his lab work; I knew I wouldn't be able to keep a straight face. Surely he wouldn't, a sex doll being in a different category from every small animal who perished on the property. But you never know with Johnny.

As he gathered his treasures, law enforcement formed a tighter and tighter circle around him. Sheriff Dane, now red-faced, was saying something. I got out of the car again, the better to hear. I was prepared to loom closer if necessary, but all I heard was, "You understand me?"

Johnny nodded and walked toward me. It was a great time to leave.

As he pulled the truck out on the highway, Johnny remarked, "I recognized the situation as a joke. Should I have laughed?"

I shrugged. "You were perfect. Someday they might start reconsidering their 'jokes.'"

"I've observed that the sheriff's department thinks I'm too meticulous. I was considering the odds that someone found the doll and said let's prank Johnny versus the doll was a personal possession and they chose this way to dispose of it. I'm leaning toward the latter because it hadn't lain outside long. Also, they stopped laughing when I talked about DNA."

I leaned back and closed my eyes. The next bump slammed my head on both the ceiling and side window. "I think you're correct."

In the silence that followed, I concentrated on predicting dangerous ruts in the road. Maybe I should keep a foam-padded baseball cap in the truck.

In a break with tradition, Johnny spoke first. "I'll send the DNA to the missing persons database. I could send yours at the same time."

I jumped and hit my head even harder. "What for?"

"Your sister is missing."

"She's not missing, and she'd be mad if the family put her photo on a milk carton when she's just off on an adventure she doesn't want Dad to know about."

"Ah. Every family is different. I sent my DNA in, as soon as I was old enough, because my sister ran away so many times. In case she didn't come back, you know, and we needed to identify a body."

"Merry isn't your sister," I snapped. I didn't say that his sister made

Cherry, the edgier twin, look like Rainbow Brite. And that made Merry a Care Bear, if there's a Responsible Bear who always plans ahead, follows the rules, maximizes for success, and never, ever would cause her loved ones any worries.

# CHAPTER 3
# JD: THURSDAY, BEAUCHAMP

We stopped by the Sonic Drive-In to report to Johnny's boss, Justice of the Peace Kevin. He thought the story of Princess Leia (RIP) was hysterical and asked Johnny to keep him in the loop on the forensic reports. He also comped our lunch order, throwing in extra tater tots, even the broccoli-cheddar kind. As you might imagine, Johnny's salary from Kevin's department is minimal and mine is nonexistent, but Sonic meals are a job benefit. The only one.

We took the food back to the office to share with Darryl and Dianne. As a starving intern and college student, Darryl appreciated the free food, one of *his* few job benefits, and Dianne didn't complain, FREE being an accountant's favorite flavor. For once Johnny and I had a justice of the peace adventure we could talk about over a meal, and I thought our audience was going to choke on their tater tots with laughter.

After my 2:00 client—one of the last ones with a free twenty-minute consultation coupon, I hoped—Johnny beckoned me into the living room-gallery-hallway. Darryl's reception desk is by the door, and towards the middle are a scattering of chairs and a sofa, all gold except for one magnificent red velvet chair. They all face the north wall, home of the big screen TV, usually covered by a Vietnamese wall hanging of cats (also in red and gold), unless someone needs to project their computer screen, like today.

Dianne lounged in the throne-like red chair, which enhanced the terra cotta undertone of her skin, toasted to a warm brown by her Mexican genes and the Texas sun. It made a shocking contrast with her little white sundress, which looked more like a short nightie with her legs extending to Hawaii.

She opened her laptop, revealing its Quetzalcoatl sticker, the bright plumed serpent god of her ancestors. I've seen client meetings fall quiet when people realize that the soft-spoken, reasonable young woman might have another side to her.

She projected yet another spreadsheet, neat and color-coded with icons. She tries to make her numbers pretty, to help people understand them. Poor Dianne.

This one was easy, with a summer timeline going across the top, and the names of las hermanas y primas, my family, and social media posts going down the left side. She was tracking Merry's contacts and social media posts, pretty sparse. Merry had posted one Doo Wop photo each week through the end of June, liked a few friends' posts on several platforms, and on July 4 declared she was going on a "digital retreat." People could leave messages on her phone, but she couldn't check it very much because of work.

"Cherry gave me the dates," Dianne explained. "She was helpful but kept saying that she was sure Merry was fine, just being independent."

"I'm sure we all hope so," said Johnny, opening his own laptop (revealing a black leopard sticker). "But I spoke with Officer Quintanilla-Villanueva about filing a missing person report. You have to initiate it, JD, and it should be done where she was last seen. However, he's willing to check the various databases and see where she or her car shows up." Johnny took control of the big screen and shared his work. "Here's her cell phone info. Her phone was indeed in Dallas in May, but it was back in Waco in June, and it hasn't moved much since then. There are two trips to Houston, one in June, one in mid-July."

Dianne frowned. "Why would she go back to Waco but not tell Cherry? Or if she did, why would neither one of them tell us? I understand about their father—maybe JD—but why not me? I mean, they called me when—" Her eyes widened and her mouth slammed shut.

I eyed her as my stomach churned. "Guys. Great job here. But is it necessary? Merry's out of touch, but she's not missing."

"We don't know, do we?" asked Dianne. "Her last contact with anyone was a text last week to Cherry, just a thumbs-up emoticon. A week before that, my youngest sister texted her to see if she'd be at the wedding this weekend. The response was

LOL no, working. 🤍🤍 to bride & groom.

We were going to that wedding because the bride was one of Dianne's cousins. Dianne was taking Johnny as her date—he thought he could almost endure it, with an extra anti-anxiety pill—and I was going to escort her next-oldest sister, because while I have the utmost respect and affection for their mother, the feeling is sadly so mutual that she never stops hoping that Dianne and I are getting back together.

Because Conchita Cortez is an awesome event planner, her whole family makes use of her talents, which means she books our band for many of those events. This time Dianne talked her into reducing our singing to a long break for the mariachi band.

"If I were a suspicious person," said Johnny, "I'd point out that sending emoticons doesn't indicate that the phone's owner sent them."

"You are a suspicious person," I said, my churning stomach now sinking as well.

I knew what they were thinking, what we all were thinking about: Lisa. Junior year in college. One of Dianne's friends, also an accounting major, who didn't show up for class one Monday. Probably sick. Or took an extra weekend day. And by the next weekend, we were all tramping through the surrounding countryside with the rest of the search team, professional and volunteer.

Okay, I could start the missing person report, just to turn up a few leads. I'd text Merry:

Ha, just checking in.

She'd text back:

Oh sorry did I forget to tell you?

That would ring down the curtain, with everyone happy.

"And you should fill out a profile for her on NamUs," said Johnny.

I stamped my feet on the wooden floor as I sat up straight. "Wait, what?"

"NamUs is—"

"I know what NamUs is. Government database to identify unclaimed remains. We're not talking corpses here. We're talking about a girl gone AWOL."

"Girls going AWOL sometimes turn into corpses," said Dianne, her eyes dark with memories.

Johnny soothed, "This is just a precaution, to be thorough. I've got some DNA kits."

Of course he did. I put my head in my hands. Reason told me both my friends were right, that no damage would be done by being prepared, and maybe there was reason to be concerned about a girl no one had seen for weeks. I stood up. "I'll get right on it."

I stalked over to my office and shut the door. Ginger Tom, the orange oyster tabby with white markings, and Gilly, the black-and-white version of his brother, spoiled my exit by demanding to come inside. They had important work to do, chasing each other around the windowsills. I don't claim any of the resident cats as mine—why bother, when they'll do the claiming?—but I have a soft spot for Ginger, whose favorite nighttime soft spot is the top of my head. That's why my brush is full of blond curls and straight orange fur.

I threw their stuffed chickens for them. Gilly grabbed his out of the air, like a good little apex predator. Ginger looked surprised when the chicken hit him on the head. I've heard that orange cats share one brain cell among them, and I don't have any evidence to refute that. But then he got to the serious business of ripping the chicken to shreds. While they rolled around, pretending to be tigers on the hunt, I gazed out to the street through the half-circle of windows in my turret. Not much moved outside, neither wind, people, nor animals. It was time to stay as still as possible until October, when temperatures would drop. Only crepe myrtles still bloomed. Their frilly blossoms lined the streets and hugged the perimeter of the house. The white ones outside my window looked like bridal lace.

Having triumphed over their toys, the cats scampered across my desk, reminding me it was time to turn to my computer and follow Johnny's good advice.

Darryl's Throwback Thursday photo was still active. I stared at the Easter photo that caught the two perpetual motion machines in permanent grins. I tried to imagine holidays and family occasions with one. How could Cherry even survive? How could I?

As I typed the NamUs URL into my browser window, I noticed how late in the afternoon it was. I'd better go file my missing person report with the police.

I was glad to find Officer Alejandro Quintanilla-Villanueva still on duty. He was one of the new hires in the Beauchamp Police Department, straight from Police Academy, still full of ideals of community and justice. We've tried to keep him idealistic. Because Johnny is assistant justice of the peace and assistant animal control officer, Officer Al often forgets that the rest of us aren't official and does a little more for us. He wasn't sure it was right for me to file a report in Alvarez County, but he agreed he could start looking in the usual places.

I spread my hands wide and shrugged. "I know, my dad should do it, but he's so in denial right now. Meanwhile, the clock is ticking."

Al's deep brown eyes were full of sympathy for my loss. "We should have reports back from the Dallas and Waco hospitals and morgues pretty quickly."

The word *morgues* shot me out of the building and harshed on my happiness. Why did everybody think she was dead?

A short time later I was back home, my arms full of dinner. It was my night to cook, usually translated as *I'll go buy something, if nobody wants my signature specialty of canned tomato soup and grilled cheese sandwiches*. I fired up the margarita machine, a parting gift from my old law firm, all of them thinking I was going to waste away drinking margaritas out in Beauchamp. While getting things to the breakfast nook table, I sang every margarita song I knew, starting with the classics from Jimmy Buffet and the Traveling Wilburys, giving a rousing rendition of "Tequila Makes Her Clothes Fall Off," and finishing up with "Besos de Fuego" as people filed in. Dianne harmonized on the chorus, bumping hips in an impromptu merengue as she wound around the table to her chair.

I waved to the table as I refilled my glass. "Fresh vegetables from our garden! Tamales from Mama Ana's truck and her daughter's famous tres leches cake! She marked some tamales with a V for you, Johnny."

"She just writes a V on them," he said, glancing at the green goo in the machine as he fetched a beer from the fridge. "They're not vegetarian."

"And margaritas for all! Except for those under twenty-one," I said to Darryl's bright expression. "Here's the virgin version."

Dianne sipped hers and choked. "You could kill fleas with this, JD." She reached for Darryl's glass and poured some of it into hers to dilute the tequila.

"Nonsense! Just like my mother used to make."

I was into my third glass and finishing up my tres leches cake when I took a deep gulp and announced, "Now I'm ready to file my sister's info on NamUS."

Dianne and Johnny exchanged looks. She shrugged and took the lead. "We already did it. I knew most of the info, and we used one of the Doo Wop photos. Anybody can post, and you didn't want to."

Johnny said, "We still need you for the DNA sample. Maybe when you're sober, though."

I poured a fourth glass, the last of the batch, and gulped it defiantly. The alcohol and ice hit me at once, and I clutched my brain-frozen head.

"You want to sleep downstairs?" asked Johnny, solicitous more for himself than me. He's done a lot of martial arts, but I'm six inches taller and thirty pounds heavier: not something he wanted to carry up the stairs.

I ignored him and took myself upstairs to bed, no problem. Okay, so I took the stairs on all fours. I still made it to bed without falling down or throwing up.

# CHAPTER 4
# JD: FRIDAY, RURAL ALVAREZ COUNTY

A fierce, bright sun sliced through my bedroom window the next morning. My phone showed me there were only minutes left in the morning, so that was a normal sun for noon in a Texas August. I had no commitments to shove me out of bed, but I felt so awful that getting up might distract me from my misery. Usually the thought of food motivated me downstairs, but not today.

By the time I got my clothes on the right way, even my shoes, and stumbled down the stairs with a death grip on the banister, everyone had eaten lunch. That suited me fine. Defying Southern etiquette, I propped my elbows on the table, the better to hold my cup of coffee, mostly for show. The contents looked like someone had mixed in a black clay soil sample, and I figured it would taste the same. I would rather have retaken the bar exam than make a new pot of coffee. So I sat and stared into the backyard and hoped everyone would think I was wrestling with a deep problem.

Instead, Johnny barreled out of the vet clinic with all his crime scene gear and said in his quiet voice, which was much too loud for me, "Good. You're up. I've got another justice of the peace call."

I took a sip of my reheated sludge. Mistake. "You couldn't go without me?"

"Of course I can." He stood there.

I sighed. "Alvarez County Sheriff or Beauchamp Police?"

"Sheriff."

I pushed my chair back and held onto the table as I pulled myself to my feet. I wasn't leaving him alone to deal with the sheriff. It couldn't end well for either of them. I shuddered, tossed back a couple of aspirin, or whatever was in the official pain reliever bottle in the cabinet by the refrigerator, and washed it down with one of Dianne's sugar-free Pepsis, showing that I was coming back to life and could make better choices than, for instance, old coffee.

Because this case was in the sheriff's jurisdiction, I wasn't surprised that we drove down more rutted country roads, though in the opposite direction from yesterday. Here, the land was farmed instead of grazed. Corn, cotton, hay, and sorghum were almost done for the year. Our destination had lain fallow, with a tractor nearby to plow in preparation for the fall crops. I longed for cold water; there wasn't a tree in sight, and hundred-degree temperatures were the norm.

Johnny hopped out of the truck with his hazmat costume in hand. I hung back to spare myself the visceral sight of a body ripped untimely from this life. I couldn't count on another sex doll. I had just heaved a slight sigh of relief that the Officer of the Day was the female deputy when a middle-aged couple approached me.

"Have they identified the body?" the woman asked. Her accent was pure Texan; her anxiety, pure fear driven by the need to know. "Pardon me. I'm Hannah Denton, and this is my husband, Buddy. We live down the road a piece, and I heard this morning at Big Tex Grocery that the sheriff's office was out here digging."

I gave my name and function. In spite of myself I looked closer at the scene of the possible crime. Instead of carnage, Johnny and the deputies stood over churned earth with bones protruding. I could handle bones, bleached of all bodily gore. The nearby tractor told the tale of an old death turned up in new plowing. This area hadn't been put to seed in a while. Depending on insects and bigger predators, the bones had lain there anywhere from a few months, minimum, to a few years, according to previous lectures from Johnny.

"Unless they find some ID, they won't know for some time." I tried to be gentle. "If you think you might know the person, tell the sheriff."

She bit her lip. "My sister disappeared nine years ago, and we've never had any leads. The sheriff's office in Deval County told us that she probably ran away. But she wouldn't have! And they never even looked for her."

It wrung my heart. No one was going to say that about my sister, not that we'd have to, Merry being perfectly fine, off on a romantic adventure, most likely. I've done the same thing, disappeared for a naked weekend. Or week. Never more than two. "The sheriff's department will want to talk to you. They'll go through their missing person reports for sure."

"My daddy filed one, but not in Alvarez County. We're in Deval County, the next one over. Will they compare notes?"

I said in a neutral voice, "If you mention it." Mostly not. Hardly ever.

Johnny joined us, and I made intros, mentioning Hannah's story.

Hannah shifted from one foot to the other. "Can you tell who it is? For nine years, my daddy's been waiting for Sara to come home, and he doesn't have much longer in this life. I—well, I want my sister back. We were best friends."

"My sympathies," said Johnny, who learned the phrase by heart after he started dealing with dead bodies. "We can't make an identification now."

Her husband asked, "Not even tell if it's a man or woman?"

"Not at this time," Johnny replied. "From the size of the bones, it could be either, and the only remaining clothes are scraps of jeans, T-shirt, and a belt, nothing identifiable. There's an old University of Texas ball cap, but that could belong to anyone. The lab will be able to tell the sex at least, and they might find a DNA match in the national database for missing persons. You could enter your own DNA; they'll look for matches right away."

"Yes! Then we'd—I'd—know for sure, at least about this person." Hannah swallowed. "Every phone number you don't recognize on your phone, you think maybe—How do I do that, enter my DNA?"

Johnny said, "I have several kits in the car. You could give me a sample now, and I'll send it in."

Her husband scowled. "Now wait a minute, Hannah. You don't want to go doing that."

"It's easy, and it doesn't hurt," Johnny assured him. "JD's going to submit a sample to help find his sister too. We can do it right now and I'll take them to the post office on the way home."

"Now wait a minute," I protested.

"You don't know what the government will do with your DNA," growled Buddy.

I raised my voice over his. "My sister is not missing."

"I saw this show where—"

Hannah broke in over her husband's words. "I'm willing to risk it, Buddy. I have to find Sara before Daddy dies."

I glared at Johnny. "This lady has been waiting for nine years, but it's a bit of an overreaction to file a DNA report for my sister at this stage."

Buddy's voice rose again. "You don't give the feds anything you don't have to. I know you want to find your sister, but—"

"I'd do anything to find her, dead or alive." Hannah's voice clogged with tears.

I insisted, "I'm just saying that—"

"We're leaving." Buddy grabbed Hannah's arm and pulled. She anchored herself and glared at him.

Johnny looked from one person to the other. His tenuous social circuits must be firing on overload. He put a hand in his pocket in slow motion. From his wallet, he drew a card and handed it to the woman. "You can contact me to keep up with the investigation. I'm not the investigating officer, but I can let you know who that is and give you any information I have. I'll be keeping up with it too."

Everyone decided at once that leaving was best.

Johnny and I didn't talk on the way back. Why should we? I'd said what I was going to say, and Johnny wasn't the type to keep after me after hearing "No" a few or ten times.

It was Friday afternoon, and nobody at Gregg House needed instruction about the evening meal. Since college, Johnny has always prepared a feast on Friday evening, his way of de-stressing from the week. In Beauchamp, that's turned into a community dinner for whoever shows up. Now that he's embracing his Jewish roots, it's a Sabbath, or Shabbat, dinner complete with wine, candles, and delicious braided challah loaves that he bakes every week. The mostly Christian town discovered that they could be accepting, when free food was involved.

My job before dinner was to chop whatever Johnny handed me, which I did, and then keep everyone's plate and glass full. My glass needed refilling more than anyone else's, but wine isn't paint-peeling margaritas, and I walked upstairs on two feet this time, though I skipped our usual Friday night movie—a few episodes from the telenovela that Dianne's family was watching. Dianne wanted to catch up because we would see her whole family at the wedding, but I was going to have to fake it.

# CHAPTER 5
# JD: SATURDAY, BEAUCHAMP

I knew no more until someone opened my door the next morning and let in four young cats. They went into some wild game on the bed, with Tabby Kee scoring the first goal by landing on my face, golden Nevada just behind her.

I couldn't remove more than two at once, and those jumped back on the bed as soon as I went for the other two. "Hey!" I shouted to the unseen door opener. "Why so early? We were going to leave for the wedding at noon."

Dianne appeared in the doorway. "Johnny says we need to visit your grandparents, the last people who saw Merry. She stopped by a week after visiting your father in Houston."

I rubbed my eyes and removed another cat. The Very Good Kitties had grown into teenage cats, bigger than the little fluff balls someone gave us at our first open house, but still technically kittens. "You didn't think to ask me?"

"Of course we did, but you were drunk. Get packed and we'll go."

I closed my eyes.

"JD."

"I am getting up," I mumbled through cat fur, as Kee settled down on my face and flipped her tail back and forth.

"We'll haul you out to the car if we have to." She leaned against the door jamb. "Remember when you went to France after your undergraduate degree? You didn't even wait for graduation."

Almost a decade later, a thrill shivered through my body. "Do I ever! When you joined me for the last month—"

"Do you remember the flight home? And the first week of law school that started the day after we got back?"

I shook my head from side to side, throwing Kee off. "Not really." I rubbed, almost scrubbed, my face with my hand. "I came home, yeah. Went to law school. What exactly?" *Home* had a funny taste in my mouth. Paris had felt like home.

"You don't remember because you were dead drunk on the plane. The crew shoved you off in a wheelchair, and I had to call Johnny to help me carry you back to Casa Cortez. The next day we pulled you out of bed and dragged you into a rideshare. I don't know how you found your classes. We kept that up—you kept that up—for a week. Every night you drank yourself to the floor, and every morning Johnny and I loaded you into some stranger's car to carry you to law school."

I rubbed my face again. "Thank you?"

"Yes, it's still a question. I still wonder if we should have let you flunk out before you started. Maybe you would've gone back to Paris, made a life there."

My heart ached. Would I ever have that life again, writing poetry on the banks of the Seine? Would I ever even get back to Paris? Or any place else out of Texas?

I must've looked as bereft as I felt because Dianne's voice grew tender. "You still could. It isn't too late. My point is that when faced with something you didn't want to do, you got drunk and stayed drunk. And now that your sister is missing, you're doing the same thing, and I swear, JD, I am not putting up with that again."

"My sister is not missing." I winced. Dianne looked like she would have thrown something if she'd had anything available.

I made a show of picking up the little cats and setting them on the floor. They, of course, jumped right back up, since I'd entered the game, whatever it was. Meanwhile, Dianne gathered steam, approaching the boiling point.

In a hushed voice, full of steel, she said, "JD, if you keep drinking,

Johnny and I will throw you out of this house, this organization. I will start procedures the next time you get drunk."

"Johnny?"

"Johnny. He and I both have alcoholics in our families. No one wants to live with one. No one wants to watch you descend into hell. We definitely don't want you to take us with you. And you might consider that you can't possibly help your sister—your sisters—if you're drunk."

I mumbled something.

She threw up her hands. "I know, I know. I hope Merry doesn't need help, and we'll all laugh about the misunderstanding. But if she does—how are you going to feel, looking back on when you could have helped but you didn't because you were drunk?"

Since the only answer was "I'll get drunk again," I was glad she swished out of the room. Nobody can swish like Dianne, even when she's not wearing a skirt.

Mad and determined to prove her wrong without wanting to admit she was right, I rolled out of bed into random clothes. I'd packed for the gig yesterday, and I had more band equipment than clothes anyway. We'd be singing in our wedding clothes instead of our ABBA suits. Beyond that, a pair of jeans and my most obnoxious T-shirt would be enough to get me to Dallas.

Going down the stairs, I stomped extra loud to let everyone know I was conscious and competent. I stopped short on the last step because a woman was standing by the vacant reception desk. Behind her, a young girl, maybe ten or eleven years old, turned in a slow circle, her purple unicorn backpack swinging side to side as she took in the nineteenth-century magnificence we called home.

"I guess you're not open today?" Hannah Denton twisted the strap of her purse.

She did that often, judging by the cracks in the plastic. She looked doughy and shapeless, but I could see the underlying determined gristle. The Stay Puft Marshmallow Man of *Ghostbusters* taught me never to underestimate someone soft and squishy; I had multiple examples of such aunties and cousins, born and bred in the South. "Steel Magnolias" has more of a ring than "Steel Marshmallows."

I looked into her faded gray eyes, the better to see the person inside. "Technically, we're not open, but we live here. We're happy to help as long as we're onsite."

"I told my husband I was going grocery shopping like I do every Saturday, but I wanted to get my DNA sent, like your partner was talking about."

I showed her into my office while tapping my phone to summon Johnny. No doubt he was scooping cat boxes in the clinic or the shelter behind the house.

"He'll be here in a minute. Have a seat." I mentally ran through the drinkable possibilities on a Saturday morning. I glanced at the three-foot antique globe that hid a drinks cabinet. No one wanted bourbon early Saturday morning, not even me. "Can I get you some water?"

She declined as she cast admiring looks at my office furniture, dark, imposing structures from the 1940s and earlier. Some came with the house; some came from Johnny's grandmother's grandparents. The girl stood behind her aunt, the better to rub the chair's red velvet with her finger and trace its channel stitching.

Curious, I asked, "How long before you started worrying about your sister? Did you think at first she'd just gone off with her friends or a new partner?"

"That wasn't the sort of thing she'd do. I was worried as soon as she didn't come home from work, but Daddy said wait a few days, that the police wouldn't do anything for forty-eight hours. I found out later that wasn't true. She was only nineteen, but she had a two-year-old, Avabella here. The daycare called me an hour after closing, when Sara hadn't shown up. She would have never left her baby there, whatever her plans were. I picked up Avabella, and she's been with me ever since." She reached back to squeeze the girl's hand and smile at her.

I shut up, so as not to trigger the tears in her voice. Johnny entered the room at that point, and I explained that she wanted to provide a DNA sample to help find her sister.

"This is her niece, Sara's daughter, Avabella," I said. "Dr. Johnny Ly."

Johnny's not interested in children of any size, but he eyed Avabella like a prize specimen sample. "Since she's here, why don't we take a sample from your niece too? A daughter reliably provides 50 percent of her mother's DNA, whereas a sibling could be 33 percent or even less, if they share only one parent."

Hannah snapped out of her tears. "I'm Sara's full sister. I don't want Avabella in some database. I just want to know if my sister's remains have been found."

Avabella tugged on her aunt's arm. "But, auntie, we might find my father too. I read this book that said DNA could tell who both your parents are."

"Your mother said we didn't need to know who he was. She didn't want him in your life. We have to respect her wishes."

Avabella's words tugged at my heart, this child who hadn't seen her mother since she was a toddler and apparently never knew her father. She was the same age now as my sisters were when our mother died. She had that same bereft expression, as though she couldn't quite believe what the world had done to her. Her best hope was learning that those bare bones in the field had been her mother. She would at least know that she hadn't been abandoned. I hoped her home with her aunt was happy, but it wouldn't be the same, would never be the same.

Johnny looked from one to the other and said, "I can take Mrs. Denton's sample now and put it in the mail. I'll give you another kit to take home in case you change your mind later."

"How long will it take to get an answer?" demanded Hannah.

"When the DNA is part of a police case, they try to move faster, in a matter of days rather than the normal weeks. JD, would you like to show Avabella our cat shelter? Mrs. Denton, come to my office."

Like any other preteen girl, Avabella was thrilled with all the cats, the scraggly, unloved denizens from Beauchamp's streets and barns that lived in our barn-turned-catitat until someone would take a chance on them. Everyone who walked into the house got a tour, in hopes they'd reduce the cat population by at least one, though Johnny advised everyone to take two.

As Hannah emerged from the clinic with Johnny, Avabella ran up to meet her aunt. "Auntie, can I have a cat? They have the prettiest orange one. Let me show you."

Her aunt sighed in exasperation. "We'll have to ask your uncle, Avabella. We can't take one today."

"But come see!"

With her niece pulling her arm, Hannah hadn't a choice.

Johnny followed to sing the cat's praises, and I followed him for lack of something better to do. The cat in question earned the label of "pretty" by having the required number of ears, eyes, limbs, and tail, too young to have lost them to the dangers of rural life. Johnny carried a small, mailing-size box in one hand. He held it out awkwardly to Hannah, who turned away. Avabella grabbed it and stuffed it into her backpack while Hannah leaned over the possible new family member.

The guests left after everyone exchanged appropriate promises, to ask Uncle Buddy, to keep in touch about the test results, and so on.

I leaned against one of the outdoor catios fastened to the barn like barnacles. One of the cats poked a paw in my ear. "I wonder whether the aunt will change her mind about testing Avabella's DNA. Very tactful of you not to point out that many families hide secrets, and Hannah might not be as close a relation to Sara as she thinks."

He beamed. "Was it? Perhaps I'm learning social skills."

"Could be. Do you think the kid taking the kit will be a problem?"

"Why would it? If Hannah changes her mind, Avabella will show it to her, saving them a trip back here. People sometimes have to get used to the idea of digging deeper."

"Oh?" I asked, deliberately ignoring any possible reference to myself.

"I've frequently noticed it," he answered, returning to his clinic and leaving me to contemplate my own state of denial.

# CHAPTER 6
# JD: SATURDAY, WACO

We took my car, because I can barely fit into Dianne's little Honda and Johnny's ancient pickup truck doesn't have enough seats for the entire band, even without Chantal. She'd been performing solo in Dallas for the past week and would meet us in Garland before the wedding. No one thought I was in shape to drive, so I ended up seething in the back seat and wishing I could figure out who I was mad at.

After Mother died, Grandfather and Grandmother Thompson sold their Houston house and moved in with us, a few miles away, to help raise the twins. Two years after the twins went to college, the elder Thompsons moved to a retirement village in Waco, because Grandmother was starting to forget things.

For now, they lived mostly independently in a little cottage. As we spilled out of the car and onto the sidewalk, we could all tell which one was theirs because of the Beethoven sonata thundering from within. I have very few memories of my grandmother not at a piano. She gave all her children and grandchildren their first piano lessons.

"That little keyboard you bought her last spring has an excellent tone," remarked Johnny as we waited for someone to respond to our knocks and rings.

When Grandfather opened the door, Grandmother wasn't sitting at the dinky keyboard I'd given her last spring. It was a baby grand, wedged into one corner of the living room, now missing several chairs.

"She spent so much time at that little keyboard, a good part of each day. I wanted her to have something closer to the sound she loved," he said in hushed tones. "It's helped her so much. Thank you, JD, for giving her back her music."

I gabbled meaningless words while Grandmother came to greet us. "JD! And your little friends! Hello, Dianne, Johnny."

I said, "We're on our way to a Cortez wedding in Garland, just thought we'd stop by to say hi to you and the twins, I hope. Have you seen them lately?"

Grandmother, her eyes bright and her voice confident, said, "Cherry has been here several times this summer. The girls always come see us every few weeks or so, but Cherry said Merry was spending the summer in Dallas."

"You forget, Arline. Merry was here in July, though it's been some weeks ago now."

I was amazed at how tender Grandfather's gruff U.S. attorney voice sounded.

A mask dropped over Grandmother's face. Her eyes looked haunted, afraid. "Did she? Surely I wouldn't have forgotten that. I do remember Cherry being here."

"She was, but earlier. Merry wasn't here very long." Grandfather patted her arm and gave me that steely look that terrified witnesses. "If you're going by the twins' place, let me give you their key. You can leave Cherry a note if she's not there. Maybe while you're here, you'd like to look around the bedroom where the girls sleep when they stay here overnight."

Johnny, not needing another invitation, headed for the spare bedroom. I accepted the twins' key from my grandfather. I knew he knew Merry was missing, and I knew he didn't want Grandmother to know.

Johnny shook his head as he emerged from the bedroom, and we made our goodbyes.

The retirement village was as far from the college as possible, and on Saturday the roads were clogged with all-day rush hour. Maybe it was

Big Game Day, although Texas highways don't need an excuse to be impassable. But we made it to the old duplex, its character and much of its structure destroyed by a succession of indifferent students. Cherry wasn't home, and I agreed with Grandfather: someone needed to go through the place. I felt bad about invading their privacy, but we had to know at least that Merry wasn't staying there.

She wasn't. No one was sleeping in her bedroom. The bed was piled high with clothes, costumes from Cherry's plays, and rejected furniture. The closet was stuffed full of winter clothes and Cherry's overflow. I duly left a note, as Grandfather suggested, but on the door, after making sure it didn't look like we searched the place.

A theory blossomed in my mind. I romanced it. "Here's what I think. Merry's back in Waco, like her phone says, but she's living with J, just not sure what her father and grandparents will think about it. So she's hiding out somewhere in some dilapidated love nest. I bet Cherry knows, though, and probably all her college friends. Should be easy to prove, no?"

"Anybody can think anything," said Johnny, not exactly encouraging.

# CHAPTER 7
# JD: SATURDAY, GARLAND

We made it to Garland, Texas, in record time, enough time to change into wedding drag at a leisurely pace. Chantal was already at the hotel. She reviewed the playlist with us as she fastened her blonde Agnetha wig—waist-length tresses for anybody else, but long enough for her to sit on—over her corn rows. I should be used to the contrast with her dark brown skin by now, but the sight always makes me blink.

"That's the point," she always said.

Besides, it's a law that ABBA tribute bands must have one female singer with long blonde hair.

Usually we wear full-blown OMG ABBA outfits, like rainbow satin suits or whatever other costume bursts forth from Chantal's fevered brain, but because we were attending the wedding first, we wanted to blend in with the guests. We could have changed clothes for the reception, but we outvoted Chantal, who admitted grudgingly that it was a short gig, so why not?

I sometimes wonder if Chantal's New Orleans background accounts for her sense of flair. Her family moved to the Houston area after Hurricane Katrina, and she came into our orbit when she met Dianne in an accounting class. I've always felt like a slacker next to Johnny, who started college at age sixteen and finished his first degree in three years, and Chantal, who graduated with a double major in music and accounting, the latter acquired for her family's sake. They worried she couldn't make a living with her singing. She's never wanted to do anything else other than sing, but she's still glad to work the tax seasons for us for the extra money.

We met my date at the church. Lourdes Bernadette Cortez is three years younger, three inches shorter, and three pounds heavier than Dianne. But though Dianne wins the beauty contest in the Cortez family, if you want to be that shallow, her sisters outshine most any other competition. Lourdes, who works with her mother, is more vivacious than Dianne. Event planners should always seem like they're having fun.

I got an unpleasant jolt when we turned ourselves over to the ushers. As cousins of the bride, Dianne and Lourdes scored seats near the front, in the third row. Johnny and I exchanged worried looks at the thought of the entire church getting to see us make fools of ourselves standing, sitting, and kneeling at the wrong time and knowing none of the hymns. I grew up in the blandest of Methodist traditions, and Johnny was raised half-assedly Buddhist and Jewish. He'd never been to a Christian service until he fell in with bad company in college, like me and Dianne.

"At least the alphabet in these books goes in the right direction," muttered Johnny, no doubt remembering the synagogue.

"Just try to find anything, though," I whispered back, shuddering at memories of Midnight Masses with Dianne's family. The church I grew up in printed the service on a single sheet. Dianne's church had a booklet that I had to leaf through for this prayer, that responsive reading, then a hymn, and so on. By the time I'd find one item, it was time to find the next one. At least this time I'd have company in my bewilderment. ·

With Chantal, Dianne, and Lourdes studying the wedding program, I surveyed the church to see how many Cortezes I could name. From taking my sisters on the clothing safaris, I recognized several female cousins and Dianne's other sisters, Tima and Juke (Fátima Lucia and Juquila Candelaria, formerly Candy) in the row in front of me.

Their brother, Zap, sat beyond Juke, way on the end of the pew near the far aisle. Their devoted mother gave her son a Marian shrine name too: Joseph Zapopan. Next to him was his date—

I gripped Johnny's arm at the same time Dianne did. He winced and then, with our encouragement, looked at the blonde, tousle-haired girl next to Zap. It was Merry. I couldn't see more than her chin when she turned to him to share a laugh, but she was my sister, no doubt, with the lavender-highlighted hair and lavender dress that promised even from the neckline to be as over-ruffled as anything Mother ever pulled over her head.

I'd carried a lead weight in my stomach since Dad's call, but I hadn't realized how terrified I was until relief flooded through me like the roaring Rio Grande River in the spring. I wanted to dance, sing, shout, but this was the wrong church for such displays. I stood up, but the organ boomed out a march, calling us all to prayer. It was not the time to leap over the pew to grab your sister. I scrunched back down in my seat.

Weddings could be shorter. Something along the lines of "You really wanna? Okay." Protestant weddings are mostly bad theatrical productions with untalented casts, but Catholics wrote the script for their wedding Masses in the dim mists of time and translated it on the fly sixty years ago. I estimated this wedding took two weeks. I did indeed make an idiot of myself, going up and down at the wrong moments and gawking at the unfamiliar parts, like the parade of older people after the wedding party—like godparents, Dianne said—and roping the bride and groom in a giant rosary, which alarmed Johnny. So between my worry and relief and trying to explain something to him that I didn't understand either, I was distracted. The incense from the swinging thurible didn't help. Its spicy scent blended with and finally overpowered all the perfumes of the congregation and the heavy floral aromas.

I counted the minutes, each as long as a month, until the priest told us, "The Mass has ended. Go in peace."

"Thanks be to God," I hollered, fervent as a convert as we fought the other Cortez cousins out of the pew. Dianne in the lead made apologies as we struggled to overtake Zap and Merry.

I wanted to kick all the lingerers out of the narthex, but Dianne continued her polite bulldozing, never stopping, even when people were so happy to see Lupita again, how long had it been, she should come home more often. Dianne kept smiling and moving until she stopped in front of Merry and Zap, nestled in a corner by a staircase, partially hidden by a nearby stand that held an urn burgeoning with peach, yellow, white, and orange smelly flowers. Johnny and I flanked Dianne on both sides to surround the two, with me next to the looming flowers and vines, ready to attack us. Chantal followed, demanding explanations.

"Merry!" exclaimed Dianne, turning it into a question before her voice died away.

"I don't think ..." I stared harder at the slender girl. Her lavender frills made her look fat as a potato, like she had as a child when Mother dressed her. I'd been so certain, looking at her from behind. Up close, I could smell her perfume, Cherry Blossom Something Something. "Cherry? What are you doing here? Is this another twin joke? Where's Merry?"

"What's the problem?" demanded Zap, just as darkly handsome as his sister was beautiful. "I asked Merry to be my date, she had to work, and Cherry offered to come in her place. She said she'd dress like Merry just for fun."

Cherry glared at each of us in turn. "Just like Merry and I have done our whole lives. And obviously he'd rather be with Merry, so I borrowed her dress."

"And got a wig that looked just like her hair." Dianne squinted at the blonde-lavender locks.

Cherry demonstrated her most theatrical sigh. She probably got an A minus for it. "Last Halloween we dressed up as each other, so I already had the wig and the outfit."

Dianne glared at her brother. "Her Instagram says she was going to Dallas to be near her darling J. Was that you, Joseph Zapopan?"

Zap flushed and scowled. "I wish! After I saw that post, I sent a DM to see if she wanted to hang out—even bring along her darling J—and she said she was dating someone, and he wouldn't understand."

Johnny spoke in his most serene voice. "We opened a missing person report on Merry before we left town."

Cherry sighed all the way to China, maybe even Mongolia. "I told you guys and Dad: she's *not* missing. She wanted to have a summer on her own. She got a job and she's working a lot of hours. They don't let her have her phone while she's working."

"When's the last time you spoke with her? Or saw her? Either of you?" asked Johnny. "Not texted, emailed, tweeted, or otherwise used any technology except the telephone to communicate with her?"

"I—" Zap's face darkened.

"I can't remember something that happens all the time," Cherry snapped.

I'd bowed out of the conversation long ago to twitch through social media. I'll spare you my expletives when I found what I was searching for. I turned my phone toward Cherry. When Dianne, Johnny, and Chantal craned their heads to see, I flashed it around. "Those photos at Doo Wop Burger, May through June. That's not Merry. It's you. I never looked hard at them, because who studies stupid selfies?"

Cherry poked her chin, pointed like Mother's, in the air. "How can you say that?"

"Because for the last twenty years my sisters thought the funniest joke of all time ended with 'I'm not Merry. I'm Cherry!' And vice versa. So I'm an expert, and I can see that little mole at your temple, almost covered by the Doo Wop hat."

Dianne and Johnny turned almost as white as me. Chantal's eyes widened. Dianne swallowed hard. "But that means—we've been thinking she disappeared ten days ago. That photo's from May. When's the last time Merry herself posted anything?"

"But she has her phone," protested Zap. He turned a ghastly shade of beige. "She's been sending texts. This morning she sent congratulations to the bride and groom on the H&P group."

I flicked through my phone. I was trying to answer Dianne's question, but a text from Officer Al popped up.

I read it silently. "I just received a cell phone report from the police. Everything coming from Merry's phone originated in the Waco area, which we knew, except for that text this morning, which came from Garland. In other words, your purse, Cherry." My stomach lurched, thrusting a nasty taste into my mouth, not helped by the carnations and ranunculus.

Cherry clutched her purse against her chest, settling any doubts.

Zap's face sagged. "Then everything from her, it was really you. How far back?"

Frowning as Cherry clamped her lips together and blinked her heavily blackened lashes, Dianne said, "I'm guessing mid-May. We need to make sure Merry at least finished the semester."

"She did!" cried Cherry. She slammed her mouth tight again as she turned more shades of her favorite color.

Johnny was wearing his internal-retreat look, where he's gone inside and processed data to come up with conclusions like: "Your father thought he'd received visits from both his daughters this summer, though never together. That isn't true, is it? It was always you."

Cherry's eyes darted around the now-emptying narthex as she searched for an escape.

Now Zap looked aghast. "Your father can't tell his daughters apart?"

Watching Cherry shrug a resentful shoulder was like looking in the mirror, the way I look when dealing with our father.

She sighed, just like me. "He could, if we were together, if it really mattered. But when Merry's phone contacts him and says she's coming for the weekend, and she shows up with fluffy curls and dressed all a-frou-frou, he doesn't question it." She tossed those curls, but in a very Cherry-ish way. "I am an actress, you know."

"So why did you willingly burn up the highway to Houston all summer to see Dad so many times?" I asked, remembering all those horrible weekends after Mother died, when I'd gone home just so the twins wouldn't be stuck alone with him.

"Duh, money, dude-bro. I make squat as an intern, and Merry didn't have a job when she left. Dad will always give you money if you shut up and go away, and I turned it into prepaid credit cards and phone minutes for Merry."

I grimaced in agreement. Chantal shook her head. The Cortez siblings looked sad, while Johnny looked like he'd just seen a set of clinical signs he hadn't encountered before.

I demanded, "So where is Merry?"

Cherry scowled.

Dianne stepped into her role of La Hermana Mayor. "We will go to the reception, and you will tell us everything. And I will ride in the car with you. You can share Chantal's and my room at the hotel tonight."

"You don't trust me!" Cherry's face matched her name.

Dianne considered and raised an eyebrow at Chantal. They shook their heads in unison. Dianne declared, "No. Not at all."

"You're not the boss of me! You don't understand."

I stepped in front of Dianne. "That's why you're going to tell us everything. And I'm appointing Big Sister Dianne the temporary boss of you. If you want to argue that I'm not the boss of you either, we'll get Dad up here to take over, and I promise he's not going to understand anything, but he is going to take action, nothing you'll like, for certain. Your choice: Dad or us, with Dianne holding your leash."

"And me as backup leash holder," offered Chantal. "But I've got to get to the reception and set things up."

She almost ran out the door. As though on cue, the disgruntled group broke up to head to the reception. I put one arm around Dianne, kissed her cheek, and breathed "Thanks" into her ear. She pressed against me for a nanosecond as we watched Johnny stroll after her charge and her brother, who must be having the worst date ever.

Remembering somebody else who must be having the worst date ever, I looked around for Lourdes. She was in the middle of the narthex, the focus of a group of admiring young men, all entranced by her sparkling eyes and laughter. I was glad someone was having a good time.

While waiting for her, I called my grandfather and told him to put me on speaker phone so Grandmother could hear. I heard him call, "Arline, JD's on the phone."

I whisked through greetings to say, "I just wanted to say that Grandmother was right. The only twin she saw this summer was Cherry, who once dressed up as Merry. She fooled everybody except Grandmother, who always knew which twin was which."

Under Grandfather's explosive "Why?" I could hear Grandmother's thin, relieved "Thank you, JD."

"You're welcome, Grandmother. Cherry's been covering for Merry so that Merry could have a summer away from us all. I'll give you more details when I know them. Gotta go."

"And that's why I didn't remember hearing from Merry," said

Dianne. "Cherry was sending all the texts, and they read like something Cherry would say, not Merry."

I pocketed my phone. "I just hope Cherry hasn't made it possible for Merry to disappear forever."

I wish somebody would have disagreed with me.

# CHAPTER 8
# JD: SATURDAY NIGHT, GARLAND

I could describe the wedding reception—tastefully, glamorously, and joyfully arranged by Conchita Cortez (assisted by Lourdes, who mostly had the night off except for running to check on something every twenty minutes)—just as it happened, but you'd find it hard to follow. So you can just imagine this conversation being interrupted constantly by the banquet; toasts that went on forever; dancing, especially La Vibora De La Mar (the Sea Snake dance, where everybody forms a big chain and prances under the arch made by the bride and groom); the devastation of the cake, which had so many layers that I got a crick in my neck looking at the toppers; and the obligatory paid dances with the bride and groom, who probably collected a down payment for a house; and, oh yes, MultiABBA giving the band a break, not to mention the band's request for Chantal and Dianne to join them for a few songs after that.

Lourdes ran off to her duties before we sat down. I glanced at my partners. Dianne bristled with happiness at being among her family again, though she moaned her way through college any time she had to return home. Chantal, the only definite extrovert among us, reveled in a new environment full of new people. Johnny, I was relieved to see, must have taken his meds or had decided he was on an anthropological safari, from the way he studied each unfamiliar aspect of the room and its occupants with a silent glee.

We grabbed a table all to ourselves as far away from the band and the food as we could get. Cherry wore a satisfied smirk, a sure indication she'd worked out her story. The kid needed to improve her acting skills. As she opened her mouth to put on her show, Johnny pulled a vial out of his pocket.

He handed it to her. "Would you spit on the cotton, please?"

Cherry gawked.

"For DNA analysis," he explained. "In addition to the police report, we filed a report with NamUs, to share with the rest of the country. JD was going to provide the sample, but it would be even better coming from her twin sister."

Cherry turned so pale that her makeup looked like a clown's face. "But that's only good if ... if she ..."

"Is dead, yes. If a set of unidentified remains turns up," Johnny said. "You have reset the game. We were looking for someone who hadn't been heard from for ten days. Now it's three months. There's a lot less hope now."

"But she's not dead! I'd know it! I'm her twin!" Cherry's tears threatened to flood her raccoon eye makeup.

"I'm not sure that's scientifically valid," said Johnny.

"Look, would you just tell us where she is and what she's doing?" I asked in my quietest voice during a break between songs, the voice I developed to penetrate a whole courtroom while giving the impression of a whisper. "I won't tell Dad if I don't need to, but I'd appreciate your easing my fears at least. I didn't know how scared I was until I mistook you for her in church."

The mariachi band filled our silence.

Cherry hunched her shoulders and leaned forward. "Okay. Last semester was bad. Really bad." She paused while the trumpet blared a solo. She took a different tack when he passed it to one of the guitars. "Merry wanted to get away by herself. I mean, you went to Paris after college."

"I did, but everyone knew I was going, and they could get in touch if necessary. Come on, it's not like our family is so close that we talk all the time. I didn't hear from anyone the whole time I was gone. If Merry had said she needed a summer retreat, Dad wouldn't have gotten worried. Me either. She wanted to get away from you too?"

Cherry nodded. "We used to do things together all the time—the same classes, the same activities. That's why Merry had walk-on parts in my plays, and I went to her environmental meetings and stuff. But we'd been doing things separately for a while, though we were still room-mates, and she wanted to go somewhere to think things out. I went to Dallas with her ID and got hired at Doo Wop Burger. She took my ID to Victoria—"

"Who's Victoria?" asked Johnny.

"Victoria, Texas. She got a mailbox there, so I could send her credit cards and phone minutes. She kept a key and gave one to me."

"Why Victoria?" asked Johnny, changing tactics.

It made sense to me. Victoria lies within easy distance of three major Texas cities (Houston, Austin, and San Antonio) and the Gulf. If Merry hadn't decided exactly where she was going, Victoria might be a good hub, though it could hardly be called a metropolis or a resort.

"She wanted to stay by the water." Cherry nibbled a Mexican wedding cookie.

"Lots of coastline near Victoria," Chantal observed. "If you don't go to Houston, San Antonio, or Austin, you end up in the Gulf of Mexico. And the coastline extends all the way to Houston and beyond.

Powdered sugar rose in a cloud and decorated Cherry's face. "She picked up a burner phone too. After about ten days, long enough for Doo Wop Burger to file her paperwork, I left the job and came back to Waco, because my internship started in June. Merry left me her real phone and told me she didn't want to hear from anybody, that I should pretend to be her and make excuses. She left early the next morning before I got up."

"So where is she now?" I asked.

Cherry shook her head. "She wouldn't tell me. I can get in touch with her if I have to on her burner phone. Look, before you do this DNA thing, let me get her to call you, so you'll know everything is okay."

Johnny nodded. "We can't get anything in the mail before Monday anyway. I have DNA from another case to send too. But you'll give us the sample now and also her mailbox key. If we don't hear from her, we're going to Victoria tomorrow, that being our only lead."

Dianne and I wiggled eyebrows at each other to determine the identity of this "we." Definitely me, and Dianne seemed to say her too.

Cherry chewed on her lip, spreading her lipstick about, adding to the black smears around her eyes and the white powder on her cheeks. "I'm going to Victoria with you."

Zap leaned in. "Me too. I tried to keep in touch with Merry, but I didn't hear anything at all after spring break, and this summer it's all been Cherry." He cast a not-exactly-angry look at Cherry, but not a friendly one either.

Johnny nodded again, implacable as the Buddha. Deep in his puzzle now, he was fine. "We would be glad to have more people to help search. But we need the DNA sample and the key now."

Cherry made an exasperated noise and wailed again, "You don't trust me!"

Unlike Dianne, Johnny didn't pause to think. "No."

I was glad to let him play Bad Cop. I patted Cherry's hand from across the table and around a vase of screaming orange carnations. "You can't blame us for not exactly trusting your judgment. With the best intentions, you let your seriously disturbed sister leave by herself, and she's been out of touch for three months. We need evidence now, not reassurances."

Cherry slapped the key on the table and spat in the vial with more force than necessary. She scowled at the three of us while she stabbed her enchiladas and rice. "She's not 'seriously disturbed.'"

Before anyone could answer, it was time to grab hold of the person nearest you and prance around the room like a sea snake, which gave us all time to calm down. When Lourdes came back from her latest overseeing, I apologized to her for being a lousy date as I led her to the circle forming on the dance floor.

"Oh, no! You must find your sister. How worried you must be! When one of my cousins ran away, we all went to my tía's house and stayed until they brought him home. Families must draw together at such times."

I smiled and thanked her as the enchiladas, fajitas, and cookies in my stomach turned to concrete. Some families stuck together; mine stayed connected at best by tenuous, wispy threads.

Cherry froze us out after that. Nobody cared. We had all the info we needed, not to mention the mailbox key and DNA sample. After gulping down a slice of cake, I gave myself over to dancing: many, many merengues, salsas, sambas, rumbas, and cha-chas, some of which I danced with Dianne. The only thing nearer to heaven is a tango with her, which she would not do in front of her mother. The tango used to be against the law, with policemen inserting rulers between a couple to keep things legal. If her mother saw us squirming against each other like that, she'd announce our engagement party, right after she dragged Dianne off to confession.

I didn't look at my phone until I was ready for bed. My heart jumped at another police text: Merry's car got a ticket on the last day of July in Lubbock, her first confirmed appearance since May. I cynically observed that Lubbock was nowhere near the beach, was nowhere near Dallas, and wasn't that close to Waco. Then I noticed something odd. The driver was Sonia Ellis. The name sounded familiar. I skimmed through Merry's social media and saw her connected to Sonia on all of them.

Probably she'd just borrowed Merry's car to go to the grocery. Probably Merry was staying with her. I'd call in the morning to confirm. There was no reason to imagine awful things. None at all.

My face must have disagreed, because Johnny said as he sat on his bed. "Would it make you feel better if I said I was sure she's all right?"

I took a couple of deep breaths that washed away all my denials. "On the basis of nothing? No. I know the odds of her being alive after this long."

"I didn't think so." He lay down and turned to the wall.

# CHAPTER 9
# JD: SUNDAY, GARLAND

I had set my phone alarm for an hour before noon checkout time, but next door Chantal was getting ready to sing at a gospel brunch. Her banging around and vocal warmups woke me earlier than I'd planned. Her goodbyes projected in her singer's voice as she left settled the matter, and I swung my legs out of bed.

Hoping my quarry wasn't a church goer, I called Sonia Ellis. She wasn't, at least not this Sunday, because she picked up right away. I was glad. Most people don't answer unknown numbers. I expected to have to borrow Cherry's or Merry's phone to get through.

I led with a cover story. The last thing I wanted to do was light wildfires of gossip and panic with news of Merry's disappearance. "This is JD Thompson, Merry and Cherry's brother. We want to give the twins a spectacular surprise twenty-first birthday party in a few weeks—"

"Oh, good! Merry's feeling better, then?"

With the wave of relief dribbling through the phone, I gave up the pretense. "I don't know. I haven't heard from her in months or seen her since the last holiday dinner. I want to give her a birthday party, but first I have to find her. Cherry hasn't seen her since May. You're driving her car—when did you see her last?"

Her voice squeaked like an adolescent mouse. "Oh no. No. It can't be. She told me not to tell anybody, but I thought she'd tell her family, at least Cherry."

My voice reflected the hollowness of hers. "Seeing as she didn't, would you feel like you could tell me? I just want to know that she's okay."

"I—I'm not sure. I—she—I know she loves you, but ..."

"I've filed a police report and set up a case with a missing persons database. We're sending Cherry's DNA on Monday. Can you make this process easier?" I swallowed hard over the lump in my throat.

A sigh trailed over the connection. "She said she wanted to go away for the summer, and she wanted to buy my van because she could sleep in it. That's what I did my first two years of college. I had scholarships for tuition, but not enough for living expenses, and my aunt gave me the van when my parents kicked me out." She took a deep breath. "For being gay."

When I didn't say anything, she went on. "We traded. She gave me fifty dollars for my van; I gave her fifty dollars for her car, which is so much better than my old clunker. We did all the paperwork, but she asked me to hold off filing as long as possible, because she was going to do the same while trying hard not to get pulled over. I guess she did better than I did. I got a ticket a few weeks ago. It's so easy to go over the speed limit with her car. My van won't even go that fast."

"Did she say why she wanted to go away?" I traced the curlicue pattern in the bedspread with one finger.

Sonia gasped. "She didn't tell you that? Everybody knew."

"Just imagine that she told me nothing, and you'll still be assuming I know more than I do."

Her voice dropped to the barest whisper. "The rape. After spring break. Those three jocks—they left her in a field out by Palestine. It took her forever to get home. Cherry took her to the hospital, and they filed reports, but the school didn't do anything. Merry couldn't bear to go to class most of the time. I don't know how she finished the semester. So she wanted to leave. She wasn't sure she'd be back in the fall, even though she had only one semester left. But she couldn't bear to see those guys ever again. I understand that. The last I saw her was in May, two

Mondays after finals. I went over to her and Cherry's duplex. We traded paperwork and cars." Her voice clogged with tears.

I coughed so mine wouldn't do the same. "Could you send me your van's information so we can track it? Did she give you any idea where she was going? Or what she might do? Did she sound like she might hurt herself?"

"I didn't think so. She said if she came back, she'd be glad to trade cars again. Oh. I guess—if? She didn't tell me where she was going, but she didn't sound like she—she did talk about the future." Sonia was silent for a beat. "I put a hundred dollars in an envelope and left it in the glove compartment for her. I didn't know if she'd have enough money to get by, and the van guzzles gas. Will you tell me if you find her?"

"I will. And let you know about the party. It's going to be the biggest, best ever." I was whistling in a pitch-black coal cellar on that one, but it seemed to make her feel better.

After she disconnected, I stared at my dark phone for a few seconds. When Sonia's car info came through, I forwarded it to Officer Alejandro and Johnny. Then I pounded the door of the connecting room. I could hear Dianne and Cherry as they opened the front door to Zap. I brushed past Dianne when she finally opened the inner door for me.

I saw red, scarlet, carmine, and fifty other shades of rage. "Are you ever going to tell us the whole story, Cherry? We've had a search going for Merry's car. Why didn't you tell us she sold it? And why didn't you tell us she was raped? Not just yesterday, but when it happened?"

Cherry faced off with hands on hips. "Because it's personal, not something you shout to the whole room, JD, like you just did."

I looked at the others, all standing with arms folded across their chests, expressions ranging from astonishment to unsurprised sorrow. "Sonia Ellis said everyone knew. Everyone?"

"I couldn't do it all myself—take care of her, go to the hearings with her, make sure she was never alone, bring her food, go to classes for and with her, even—" She caught her breath. Her face turned some of the colors I was feeling. "You want me to tell you everything? Okay: I took one of her exams for her. She couldn't get out of bed. I didn't want her to flunk out, and I thought I could pass the test because I'd helped her study. Not that I did her any favors. I got a C minus. But at least it was a passing grade. When I told her, she dragged herself to the rest of her exams."

In the silence, Dianne said kindly to Cherry, "We try not to do illegal things around JD, or at least not tell him. We never know what he might have to report, being an officer of the court."

"That's not the kind of thing I have to report." I lashed my brain and tied it to my mouth. "You didn't think I could help? How did you manage everything?"

She wailed, "I keep telling you, she didn't want you or the rest of the family to know. You? She said she'd die if you knew. I pretty much believed her." Her voice cracked.

I didn't know what to say, but I figured anything would be wrong. I did manage to close my mouth.

Dianne's eyes drilled into mine as she explained in a flat but still kind voice, "Talking about rape is reliving it."

Johnny said from behind me, "That is very true. Most people don't care to."

Eyes wide, I whipped my gaze from Johnny to Dianne. I'd gate-crashed a #MeToo meeting. My friends—they'd never told me.

Johnny turned to Cherry. "Did you know about the car, though?"

It was Cherry's turn to sound worried. "No. I worked at Doo Wop Burger in her name to get her into the New Hire database, in case anybody seriously looked for her. She thought they—you know, those guys—might come after her. Maybe she was paranoid, but she was determined. When I got back from Dallas on the Sunday night before she left, her car was in the driveway. I got up late the next morning, and she was gone. She left a note saying she couldn't bear to say goodbye. I thought she drove off in her car."

Finally I had some facts to report. "Sonia Ellis said she drove to your place on a Monday morning and swapped cars. I gave that info to the police. And Johnny."

Zap's voice was as taut as a guitar's high string. "Shouldn't they be doing more? Put her picture on the news? The media likes stories about beautiful missing blonde girls."

"She's not blonde anymore," said Cherry. "She colored her hair the morning she left, some kind of dead mouse color. I found the bottle in the trash."

"And she might be a ginger by now," said Johnny, as he put his phone away. "Merry has a grasp of basic disappearing."

"Should we leave it to the police and the media?" asked Dianne. "What can our team do? She wanted to go to the coast. There's over three thousand miles just in Texas, and another three thousand along the Rio Grande, if she'd settle for a river."

"Cherry, you were going to ask her to call me. How'd that work out?" I swear, I was trying for a neutral tone.

Cherry shook her head, maybe to sling the tears aside. "I texted—no answer. I called—no voicemail. Actually, it sounded like the number wasn't even in service. I sent her more phone minutes just a week ago."

"Maybe she got a new phone. Don't the disappearing gurus say to keep changing phones?" asked Johnny.

"But she'd tell me!" said Cherry with an edge of desperation.

"Like she told you about the car swap," I said, neutral as I could be.

"What did the car matter? She promised she'd keep in touch. She's my twin!" Cherry's next stop was full-blown hysteria, and nobody had even mentioned the possibility that Merry might not have had a choice.

Taking the role of the Official Hopester, Zap said, "Maybe she sent you a letter."

Cherry seized it. "That's it. I'm definitely going to Victoria with you, but we can stop in Waco and check my mail."

Johnny, Dianne, and I had one of our silent meetings of flickering gazes and micro-expressions in our Orchid-ese language. Johnny announced our conclusion: "That seems sensible. We'll make a decision after we see what's in Waco and Victoria."

After we decided on who was riding in which car, Zap handed out the donuts and kolaches he had brought for a late breakfast. Johnny brewed horrible coffee in the hotel coffee makers, and Dianne and I loaded the cars.

The plan was that I would drive my car, Johnny would drive Cherry's (to be left at her duplex in Waco), and Cherry, Zap, and Dianne would ride in Zap's car. I wasn't sure what he thought he could do, besides bring donuts, but he insisted on going. Dianne scolded him about leaving his romantic dreams in the deep freeze until Merry had a chance to heal. He replied indignantly that he wasn't such an idiot as that; he knew lots of assault survivors.

I watched and listened through a fog. It occurred to me, not for the first time, that life sucks.

As I slung my suit bag into the trunk, I asked Dianne without looking at her, "I'm not going to ask you what happened."

"Bueno, amigo. Because I am not telling you, not without multiple jeroboams."

I stuffed my fists into my pockets. "I hope I never made it worse for you, brought back memories, that sort of thing."

When she didn't say anything and I didn't hear any car doors or trunks, I snuck a look at her, standing by Cherry's car while she leaned on the handle of a rolling suitcase.

She took a deep breath, her chest rising and falling. "No."

It's good to talk these things out.

# CHAPTER 10

# JD: SUNDAY, GARLAND TO VICTORIA

Bags were not being loaded. Dianne shook herself and tossed Johnny's suitcase into the trunk. She threw her own bags after it. "Zap will be okay with Cherry. She won't charm him into going rogue. I'm going to drive your car because your life taco just got stuffed to overflowing with too much reality."

"What about your life taco?"

"My life taco has been full of such ingredients for years."

I made some kind of sound that was meant to be a protest. Then I said, "Thanks."

Our caravan set off south down I-35, along with everybody else in Texas. I've observed before that every vehicle drives up and down I-35 on Sundays from the northern to southern border. At least we were starting a few minutes early.

I both wanted and didn't want to talk to Dianne. At first, the remaining kolaches from Zap's breakfast took care of the problem, with her swilling her eternal sugarless Pepsi and me rejecting the hotel coffee for a bottle of water. Then I cranked my music and sang with it all the way to Waco, with Dianne on harmony.

When we joined the other car, Cherry's shoulders drooped further when she found nothing but bills in her mailbox. Zap said she had run the battery down on her phone, texting and dialing Merry's burner phone. We left Cherry's car at her duplex and took Johnny into my car.

We jumped back on I-35 and crawled our way to Austin, where lunch was a quick swish by our drive-throughs of choice. Johnny was annoyed that the Vegetarian Special at a burger joint turned out to be not a soy patty, but a standard hamburger with all the trimmings, except the burger itself. For an upcharge, he got a few more pieces of cheese to make it almost edible. Dianne let me drive at that point, while she pulled out her laptop, one of her coping mechanisms.

Once we abandoned I-35 to wander through more rural areas on Highway 183, we saw that August had parched the countryside, leaving even the sunflowers limp and the livestock immobile by their ponds. Corn fields had shriveled to husks, and giant rolls of dry hay lay in the fields. "Jelly rolls," the twins used to call them. The sun baked our arms and thighs too, as it streamed through the windshield. The air conditioner couldn't help that.

My car pulled in first to Merry's post office. I had the key, but we waited for the others to arrive. Cherry shoved the others aside, making sure she stood right next to me as I turned the key.

I had trouble getting the door open, like something was stuck in the lock. Many things were: multiple cardboard Priority mailers, bent and mangled.

Cherry gasped. "She never came! Those are the things I sent her. They're full of credit cards, phone minutes, gas and grocery store gift cards. She never picked them up!" She ended in a full shriek.

Zap and Johnny each took one of her arms. They half guided, half carried her out the front door. While Cherry sobbed outside, Dianne and I pried the mail loose. Dianne being Dianne, she insisted on sorting the mail in chronological order before leaving the post office. That seemed preferable to trying to comfort my sister, now that she'd joined the rest of us in dreading that we'd never see Merry alive again and maybe not dead either.

Zap wedged Cherry back into his car, but in the backseat this time, where she still sobbed, though quieter, on Johnny's shoulder. He stared straight ahead, his expression rigid, while he patted Cherry's shoulder with his opposite hand and said, "There, there"—the script I wrote for him when we first moved into Casa Cortez in college with enough women to field a baseball team.

Dianne opened the back door and said, "Chica, you need to help us. The earliest piece of mail is from the first of July. Did you send any earlier?"

Cherry rooted around in her purse. I thought she was looking for a tissue, but she pulled out a handful of post office receipts. "I went home at the end of May as Merry, got money from Dad, mailed it after Memorial Day. Two weeks later, in the middle of June, I went home and got some money from Dad, as me this time. I turned it into prepaid credit cards and phone minutes and mailed them on the next Monday. Those two are gone."

"Any contact with her?" asked Johnny.

"She sent texts. Well, somebody did." She showed us a phone screen full of one-word and emoji texts in response to Cherry's messages, the last one three weeks ago.

Dianne traded a few soft words with Johnny and then headed for my car. I followed to get drinks from our ice chest. But as I gathered bottles of tea, water, and Pepsi, Dianne put her hand on mine and shook her head. "We passed a café on the previous block, the Texas Rose or something like that. Let's go there and figure out what to do next. It's too hot to stand outside or sit in a car."

I put the drinks back and slammed the trunk shut. I looked straight into her light brown eyes with their dark rings and golden flecks. "Remember when we went searching for Lisa, us and half of Austin?"

She muttered a Spanish obscenity, which I strained to hear because I always want to improve my vocabulary. "Like I wouldn't? She was my friend. She lived with us one semester."

"Did you think we were going to find her alive?"

She paused long enough for all her emotional doors to slam shut. Her face looked blank, her eyes hooded. "I thought she was in a Schrödinger's state, neither alive nor dead, and we had to find her to make her one or the other. I hadn't much hope, but dead would have been better than unknown." She turned her back on me as she climbed in the car.

I dawdled, wanting to quit this scene but not wanting to go

anywhere else. When Zap honked his horn, I eased into the driver's seat and followed him.

I parked on the side street under Texas Rose's mural of huge yellow roses. The sign swinging over its striped awning read THE TEXAS ROSE CAFÉ AND ICE CREAM PARLOR. It filled me with dread. I hoped it wasn't going to look like Houston's The Sweet Shoppe, a vintage-looking ice cream parlor full of pink stripes, ruffles, and chairs with curly-wire backs. Cherry and Merry spent most of their childhood celebrations there. I can still see them bouncing, bubbling with excitement and sugar after dance and piano recitals, plays, sports events, report cards, first and last days of school—they never wanted to go anywhere else. It was certainly no place I'd ever choose to go, but I like to think I did better than my father, who visibly steamed during such outings.

I let out a sigh when we walked inside. Rather than Terminally Girly, the vibe was Ye Olde Wilde West. I saw a few decorative chairs with curlicue backs, but the floor looked like original wood, uneven and splintered, and the booths looked like they sprang from the same source. The walls were the same brick as the outside, with garish posters of long-ago shows. Cherry, already seated in a booth beside Johnny, seemed not to notice at all, her gaze going straight through the poster of a dancing girl in a red-flounced dress and black lace garters.

Dianne slipped in by her brother, and I sat next to her. I liked being on the end, like I was separate from the group. I got up and pulled one of the dainty chairs to the end of the booth after Dianne's elbow poked me a few times as she wrestled her computer open. Cherry flinched away from Quetzalcoatl's raging visage on the top, now facing her.

With a grim smile at Cherry's response, Dianne tapped a few times and turned her laptop around to show her updated spreadsheet to everyone. "This shows all the contacts anyone's had with Merry since she left. Except now we know that Cherry made most of them, indicated by the pink cells."

"It's practically all pink," objected Cherry.

"Looks like you went home to Houston every two weeks, alternating personas," I said.

Cherry sniffed. "Could you stand Dad more often than that?"

"Not that much," I replied. "You should get a medal."

The waitress brought water and took our orders, King Ranch Chicken all around. There must be a law on the books that says you have to order King Ranch Chicken whenever it's on the menu. It's one of those I-Own-Only-One-Pot dishes, a combination of meat, tomatoes, peppers, onions, soup, and two kinds of cheese on top. It's named for the famous King Ranch along the Rio Grande, but for no reason other than marketing. When my grandparents were children, they thought it something special when it appeared on their school lunch menus.

Everyone at this table looked happier in the anticipation, even Johnny, who would pick out all the chicken and pass it to someone else.

"As I said," Dianne reiterated. "The last time anyone saw her was two Mondays after finals, when she and Sonia swapped cars. Cherry saw her the night before. Since then, Cherry's received some texts that dribble down to emoji by July. We can't assume they're from Merry even though they came from her burner phone. The last text Cherry received was July 30, some weeks ago now. We know someone picked up the mail in June, but not since. All we know of her plans was that she hoped to stay on the coast. JD, you sent the burner phone info to Officer Al. Have you heard from him?"

While I shook my head, Johnny said, "I brought our own phone-tracking software, and I checked it."

"So what did it tell you?" I asked.

"Nothing."

"Nothing? As in—"

"As in her phone doesn't show up anywhere."

"She probably keeps it off most of the time," offered Zap.

"That wouldn't matter. Most phones, even cheap ones, have GPS software. You have to take the battery out to turn it off," Johnny declared.

That sank our spirits below sea level.

# CHAPTER 11
# JD: SUNDAY, VICTORIA

"What do we do now?" asked Zap. "If I can't get back in time for work tomorrow, I need to let them know."

"We have to find her!" Cherry cried.

Johnny had brought in a folded paper map. He snapped it open hard enough to tear it at the folds. It must have been in the car for years. He folded it to show only the relevant area and pointed. "If she picked Victoria as a mailing address, she wouldn't want to be hours away."

"Good point," agreed Dianne. "It takes two hours to get to any big city from here. Are you going to ask the police to search the hospitals and such in those places? They can do it faster than we can."

I glanced at Cherry to see if she interpreted *such* as *morgue* like I did.

Johnny got busy with his phone. "She grew up in Houston, but I don't know whether that would make her more or less likely to go there. Probably not Austin. If she didn't want to come to us, she wouldn't want to be where we might see her. Does she have any connection with San Antonio?"

"I can't think of any," said Cherry. "We should get on the road. She wanted to stay by water, but there's a lot of coastline."

"Three thousand miles of it," I agreed. "And that doesn't include bays, lakes, and other inland bodies of water."

"We need to narrow down the possibilities. It would take most of a day to drive to all the cities I mentioned." Johnny sipped his tea. "I have patients in the morning, so I can't do much more today."

"I have tax clients," said Dianne.

"You're all horrible. You don't care what happens to my sister," Cherry complained as she stabbed chicken chunks.

Ignoring Cherry's outburst, Dianne asked, "JD, what do you think?"

I wanted more time to think—or at least to keep stirring the King Ranch sauce over its cheese—but Cherry was headed straight for a breakdown of Wagnerian operatic proportions. "Cherry's right. We need to look. But Johnny's right, too. We need a plan, even a bad one. Merry wouldn't try to hide among us, so we can cut out the Austin area. If she went to San Antonio, we don't have a clue about where to start, and it's a huge city."

"And nowhere near the water," muttered Cherry.

I continued, "So I vote for Houston, where we grew up. It's near the coast. Merry would know how to hide in plain sight and never run into people who would care. If she saw anybody she knew, she'd give the 'Just visiting for a few days' speech, and they'd never think about it again, because that's the relationship we all had with our hometown after we'd gone away to college. And what's close by? Galveston Beach, where we went every year for summer vacation."

I recalled many pilgrimages to the beach, memories stacked like plates. Me as a kindergartener, bringing my mother beach treasures: shells, sand dollars, beer cans, and used condoms. Me helping Mother chase my baby sisters from toddlers to tweens. I'd rather have been hanging with my friends and applying suntan lotion to girls' backs, the most exciting sexual experience I would have for some time. But Mother had cancer by then and often said, "JD, can you look after the twins?"

I always did, as though that would make her well.

I rubbed my forehead, as though that would erase the memories. "I don't have to be in court next week, and I can reschedule appointments or handle them remotely. I'll swing through Houston, look through the house, talk to Dad and your friends, and then head for the coast. I need you to make a list of friends that Merry might have confided in or at least run into and any place from the Galveston area that might be important to her."

"Dad? No way! You can't tell him!"

"I never tell Dad anything I don't have to. But look at what we know: Merry picked up your mail in June but not July, and she knows how to work Dad like you do. What if she went to Houston toward the end of June and got such a large sum of money that she didn't need to keep going to Victoria? I need to get the dates Dad saw Merry this summer and compare them with the dates Dianne has on her spreadsheet."

"And you seriously think Dad will remember the dates he saw one of his darling daughters this summer?"

"Of course not. But his bank account will, and if he gave out money on a date you weren't there, that will tell us more about Merry's activities."

"He could have given her a credit card," Dianne observed, eyes gleaming with the financial chase, so dear to her forensic accountant's heart. "And the dates and locations on it would tell us even more. See if your dad will let me examine his records."

"I will, but not likely." To Cherry's disgruntled expression, I added, "Look, maybe the van died and she asked for help to buy a new car. He'd remember that."

Cherry sniffed. "Why wouldn't she have told me?"

That was the crux of the matter. We're an imaginative bunch. We could come up with explanations for Merry's actions, but not her silence, not from her twin. The waitress broke our collective dread to ask if we wanted anything else.

Cherry's voice rose in pitch and reverted in years. "Can I have a strawberry ice cream soda?"

"No," I replied automatically. I mentally shook myself out of teenage-JD mode. "What am I saying? You're twenty. You can have anything you want."

"Whipped cream and a cherry, please," she specified. Her expression grew sadder after the waitress left. Still in her little girl voice, she asked, "JD, why is Dad such a dick?"

I caught myself before I delivered one of my standard zingers. She'd asked sincerely. "I don't know, but his wife had cancer for five years before she died and left him with two young girls to raise."

"Grandma did that. Raised us. Are you saying before Mommy got sick, he was all lovable like a TV dad?"

I thought back to my earliest days. "I'm not saying that. He and I never got along. I wasn't the son he wanted. He wanted me in sports; I wanted to play music. Remember how mad he was when I made the basketball team freshman year and wouldn't play the year after? It took up too much time, especially with Mother sick."

"Not really. He was always mad."

"You would have been six or seven, so I'm not surprised." I let the memories flow for a minute and then said, "People always said we were too different, Dad and me. But what if we were too much alike? What if he wanted to play music and write poetry but he couldn't because he was expected to Be a Man. Words were for winning, like in a courtroom, not for beauty, gentleness, healing, joy."

Expressions of disbelief surrounded me, with Cherry as Disbeliever-in-Chief. "Just not feeling it, JD. That's not the Dad I know." Now in possession of her soda, she sucked her cheeks in hard, as though to empty the glass in one gulp.

"It's hard," I admitted, dipping my spoon into the ice cream Dianne pushed my way. She'll order dessert if she can share it, in this case, with Johnny and me. "Don't worry. It'll be years before I try to be fair to him again. Today I'll check out your friends, anybody she might have gone to or confided in. I'll go to the house tomorrow while he's still at work. I want to search our bedrooms, if you don't mind, in case Merry left a clue. Then I'll head to the coast. Do you remember any place she particularly liked?"

Cherry shrugged one shoulder. "You always went with us. You'd know as much as me."

I gritted my teeth. "We stayed at a different place almost every year. Did you two like one more than the other?"

"The blue one. On stilts."

All coastal cottages were built on stilts, in hopes they would survive the hurricanes. Those that weren't blue were green. Or blueish green, evoking the water.

Mother loved the beach but avoided the major tourist attractions, like Galveston and Padre Island. We spent many summer days in a beach cottage, with Dad joining for an occasional Saturday. Once after Mother's diagnosis, my fifteen-year-old self complained that Dad was never around to take care of his little brats who were making my life miserable.

"Fine, then. We'll just go home and stay there." He smiled in triumph at his brilliant solution.

The light faded in Mother's pale blue eyes. I left the room to find the twins.

When I did, I hiss-whispered at them, "If you don't want to go home forever, you'll get in there and pull a twin-bomb on Dad and tell him what angels you'll be—and you'd better be—if he'll just let us stay here longer."

While they grabbed his hands and howled about the unfairness of it all, including promises of repentance, I called Grandmother and got her promise to join us in a few days. That gave my dad a graceful way out— totally out, because he drove back to Houston that night. The twins mostly kept their promise, and Grandmother was a great help to all. That was the first time the twins and I ever worked together. Maybe the last time until now—if we were. I guess we weren't, because Merry wasn't here, might not ever be again.

I tried again. "Anything in particular you liked to do?"

"Oh yes! One or two times we stayed in a cottage with an elevator, and we liked riding it, playing games like sending things up and down, one of us on the ground floor, the other on the top."

I smiled in a way that felt like a wince. We had stayed in the elevator cottage—same one, two years in a row—when Mother was too weak to climb stairs.

Cherry sank into happy memories. "And the last year—remember? —we stayed in a real hotel, historical and everything, really in Galveston instead of the podunk Nothingvilles. It was right next to those blue pyramid things. You took us there every day, and it was *so* far to walk."

"We took the tram," I mumbled as I looked down, pretending to scoop the melted ice cream.

Three months after that trip Mother would be dead. Because she had wanted to go to the beach one last time, we stayed in the Hotel

Galvez and Spa, with all possible amenities and accessibility, in a big town near a hospital. And Moody Gardens, the blue pyramids Cherry remembered.

Mother's eyes were clouded with drugs and pain much of the time, and Grandmother grew expert in recognizing the right time to say, "JD, why don't you take the twins to the gardens?" I did, because there wasn't anything else I could do to help, but I wanted to stay with Mother. It didn't take a doctor to see she wouldn't be with us much longer.

Still trying not to show those memories, I said in measured tones, "Send me contact info for your—her—friends from high school. I'll give them the same story I used for Sonia. 'We're planning a big twenty-first birthday party for the twins at the end of the month, no details yet, just saving the date, trying to figure out the best venue. Don't let the twins know. Have you seen them lately?'"

Cherry attacked her straw one last time with a raucous slurp. "But I'm going with you."

"Are you? You have work on Monday." I eyed her. I judged her mental-emotional state as more than halfway to blown.

"God, JD. How can I work when my twin is missing?"

"Your twin has been missing since May. The only difference now is that you know about it." I felt like someone was staring at me. I glanced sideways to meet Dianne's gaze.

She understood my problem immediately. A rush of love for her washed over me, but I tried not to take it seriously. It's not like Johnny didn't know me well enough to reach the same conclusion.

In her most soothing voice, she asked Cherry, "Chica, what will you do if you go with JD?"

"Whatever he does. I have to find Merry." She pulled out her phone again to send yet another text. She tried to call, and when she got no response, slammed the phone on the table.

Dianne continued, still soft and low, "Cherry, JD has a plan. Do you? What can you do that he can't? Will he have to spend his time taking care of you instead of searching?"

"It's not fair! I should look for Merry. I lost her. And don't say I should go to my stupid intern job and run the copier until it breaks. What does it matter?"

Dianne nodded. "I certainly understand, but I suggest you go into the office on Monday, tell them about Merry, and let them see what a wreck you are. Then, when they tell you to go home for a few days, protest your loyalty to the firm, declare your willingness to serve, break down, and finally accept their generous offer."

"You'd do that?" asked Cherry, skeptical.

"Not exactly. Not wanting to be called *that spicy Latina*, I never showed an emotion at work. In a situation like this, I'd claim I had to go home to support my family. *You* can be as emotional as you like. If you have a weekend phone number, you call them today. Just don't blow up your life by quitting."

"That makes sense, Cherry," I said, trying not to show my relief. "All the reasons you took that job will still apply next month, next year, and beyond. And going to work will give you something to do while you wait, which is the hardest part."

The long-held tears burst out, streaking down her cheeks to plop onto the table. She laid her head on her arms. "I just can't go back to Waco and act normal. Not when my sister could be dead."

Dianne placed a hand on the blonde curls across the table from her —still Merry's curls, not Cherry's angles. "We don't know she's dead. We hope she's not. You don't have to get an early start on your mourning. If you can get time off, you could come stay with us in Beauchamp while you wait. You can help our intern. There's plenty of work to do. What you will not do is lie around and mope. You need to keep busy."

While I blinked in awe at Dianne inviting my grief-torn sister into our house, Johnny, of all people saved the day. "Taking care of the cats is soothing. And I can show you ways to help search for your sister remotely."

Zap, who'd been staring anywhere but at my family, offered, "It's not like you'll be out of touch or like this arrangement is forever. I'm sure your brother will call often, and you can make other plans when necessary."

Cherry started a sniff that turned into a snort. She wiped her cheeks and nose with the dainty napkin provided by the Texas Rose. "I guess."

Dianne motioned for the check. "So we're all going to Beauchamp? Zap will return to Dallas from there and JD will go to Houston?"

I stood and threw some bills on the table for my share of the food. "No, I'll save myself a few hours of driving, the better to start searching sooner, and head east to Houston from here. Anything I need, I can buy."

The flickering glow in Cherry's eyes almost made up for the grumbling disquiet in my heart.

# CHAPTER 12
# JD: SUNDAY, HOUSTON

Relieved to go on my journey alone, I waved goodbye as they and their baggage all piled into Zap's car. Then my heart sank. I was going on my journey alone. Was that what I wanted? For three seconds I contemplated driving in the opposite direction until I was out of gas. I would like to think mature consideration stopped me rather than the fact that I'd run out of gas in fifteen miles.

While I filled the gas tank, I planned my next move. I called my father from the gas station. Judging from the background noise, he was playing racquetball. Judging from the foreground noise, he was annoyed.

"I won't keep you," I said. "I'm not having any luck finding Merry, and I wondered how many times you've seen her this summer."

"I told you previously, once a month or so. What does it matter to you?"

That tracked with Dianne's spreadsheet. "So nothing out of the ordinary? You didn't buy her a new car or anything on that level?"

"What's wrong with her car?"

"Nothing that I know of. I just wondered if you made any unusual purchases for her or gave her more money than usual.

"I repeat, what do you care?" he asked amid the balls slamming against gym walls.

"I'm trying to find her, and I don't have any place to start."

"Did I ask you to do that?"

"Didn't you? Wouldn't I anyway, once I knew she was missing? She's my sister. I filed a missing person report—"

"How dare you! You had no right to do that. I'll do it, if it's necessary."

I took deep breaths. "You know what, Dad? It is necessary. Cherry hasn't seen Merry since May and hasn't had even a text from her for weeks. I haven't talked to her since spring break, Dianne and her family either. I filed the report in Beauchamp, and they'll be happy to turn over what they've found—rather, haven't found."

"JD, stop meddling in what doesn't concern you. I'm her father, and I'll decide what and when—"

I held the phone toward the highway, the better to pick up the traffic noise. "Sorry, Dad. Breaking up. Can't hear you."

Well, that was normal. Back on the road, I cranked up my music and sang along, even the instrumental parts, even when it sounded like HEEK Horka Hork Kah Kah Kah because it was better to have that in my brain than my father's words and what I shoulda coulda woulda said back. After a few ABBA tunes and some growling poetry from Leonard Cohen, one of my favorite singers because he sings in my range, I attained some kind of mellow state by the time I reached the outer limits of Houston. Music makes me happy.

By the time I turned into West University Place, a little township near Rice University, I could admit—fleetingly, once—that far in the back of my mind I had been hoping my father and I could work together on something, something important to us both, to make up for a long childhood of me trudging out to the driveway to shoot hoops with him on his demand.

Stupid idea. He didn't speak to me for a month after I dropped out of basketball freshman year, and I'm sorry he ever started again.

Originally, I'd planned to contact the twins' friends that evening, but I hadn't received the list from Cherry, so I drove by the house in hopes of starting my search there early. I planned to keep driving if I saw Dad's car, but the two-story vintage white brick house, all spiffed up for market, sat dark amid its livelier neighbors. Dad would have gone out for dinner and drinks with his buddies after racquetball. I probably had a few hours before he returned, and I could always claim that I wanted to spend the night. But I didn't want to talk to him again, so I parked on the next block. I promised myself I'd keep him updated on my search— by text.

Last year Dad swore he was selling the house and told us kids he'd throw away anything we left behind. I rented a dumpster and a moving pod last summer, and Merry, Cherry, and I spent weeks rescuing our treasures, quite a few of my mother's things too. Then he didn't sell the house, claimed the other party backed out at the last minute. He said there wasn't a rush. With the market going up, he would wait for the right opportunity. Meanwhile he had a perfectly clean stage-ready house.

What Merry and Cherry didn't take back to school with them, I put in a storage unit. Yes, I was still mad about Dad's trick to get us to scrub the house of our presence. So when I came home, it was to a stark structure that looked nothing like my childhood home on the inside. On the other hand, it should be easy to tell if Merry had left anything behind. In twilight's last gasp, after turning off the security system—same password as when it was installed—I searched the grounds for the secret hiding places where they left notes for each other and their friends. The apartment over the separate garage had never been rented. We kids gave our parties there, but it was bare, not even a stray Coke can.

The same was true for our bedrooms, now just furniture, no secret hiding places. I didn't find anything in the rest of the house either. Except for the graduation photos over the mantle, you couldn't tell Dad had daughters. Or a son. And those could've been staged to make the house look like a family house, though there were no photos of the family, not even of Mother.

That made me mad. I entered that *sanctum sanctorum*, his bedroom. I hadn't gone in there since it became his bedroom only. The only artwork on the walls might have been stolen from a hotel; nothing graced the dresser or the nightstands. It didn't look like anyone lived in this room either. That made me mad. I had told him last year that I wanted anything of Mother's that he didn't, no matter what it was. Photos were top of the list, and I remembered a huge portrait of him and Mother on their wedding day, and nineteen sixteen-by-twenty-inch photos of the family as it grew. Dad hadn't had any made after Mother died, though we kids had our obligatory graduation photos, the ones hanging over the mantle.

As I flicked off the room's light, something made me decide to look in the closet. In the far corner of Mother's side, the quilt her mother made hid twenty of those missing portraits. A smaller one lay face down on top of the drawers in the closet: Mother's engagement photo. My heart clenched at the breezy young beauty of this woman I'd never known, younger than my current age, probably in her last year of her master's degree. Best that she not know what lay ahead: cancer, death, and a husband doing his best to erase her memory.

Tires on the driveway interrupted my rage and maudlin reflections. I congratulated myself for having shut off lights when I finished searching each room and shutting the closet door before turning on the light. I clicked off the closet light and crept back to my own room by the light of the street lamps. My room might now be as bleak as an institution, but there was one thing he couldn't take away from me.

I hoped not, anyway. No one thought the second-story windows needed alarms. Though the white paint was new, surely he wouldn't have had the windows painted shut. I waited until I heard the back door rattle before trying to raise the window. It lifted smoothly. I slung one foot over the sill and tested the roof of the enclosed back porch. Okay, not everything was the same.

Instead of encountering the rough shingles of my teen years, my foot slipped on smooth metal. From a homeowner's standpoint, that made sense, to convert your inexplicably crumbling roof (thanks to your sneaky teenagers) to sun-repelling metal. From my standpoint, that act rendered the few steps to the thick branches of the oak tree a perilous hazard. I might fall. Even worse, I might be heard, and I didn't think Dad would put the metal popping down to a super-grande-size squirrel.

While I tested the roof under my foot, I listened for sounds that would tell me where he moved through the house. Did he notice that I'd disarmed the security system? Didn't seem to, or just figured he forgot to set it. It was one of the older, stupider models. He barely paused before continuing through the house. To his office or the den? Computer or TV? TV noise would give me more cover, but his office was farther away from my perch over the back porch. If he went to the den, I could expect to hear the TV in 5—4—3—

The kitchen phone rang. I froze. Footsteps resounded through the house, from the den, I guessed, judging by the number of steps it took him to reach the kitchen. Who has a freaking landline anymore? Is that even allowed? I had the best seat in the house if I wanted to eavesdrop, but I didn't care who he was talking to on a Sunday night.

He barked a greeting, but his voice got quieter. Not intimate quieter, like a lover, but not someone he was confronting or angry with. That being the case, he didn't have much to say, though still enough that I had to shift my position. The roof popped, but no louder than a plus-sized raccoon.

Dad ignored it. The refrigerator door opened. I groaned in silence. He'd just had dinner and he needed a snack? Maybe just a beer. Nope, getting a drink wouldn't take that long. Good grief, did he need a cheese board, a charcuterie plate, crudité, and a partridge in a pear tree (lightly glazed and roasted)? I ruled out the office. He wouldn't eat over the keyboard.

I held still until his steps faded. Then I dared to put both feet on the roof and wiggle around. I eased the window shut, most of the way, anyway. Shouldn't trigger security, if there was any.

If I pressed right up against the house, where the roof was fastened, I wouldn't make the roof pop. I hoped. I was glad for my running shoes. They didn't slip on the metal as badly as dress shoes would have. The porch roof sloped slightly so that water wouldn't pool on it, but nowhere as much as a standard house roof. I could do this. I took a sideways step. Then another.

I had to let go of the window frame. It wouldn't hold me if I fell. Deep breath. Two more steps to the tree and pray the limbs hadn't been trimmed recently.

They hadn't. I eased myself into the welcoming branches. I paused for a sigh of relief as I let the intersection of branch and trunk cradle me. I wondered if my sisters had used the same escape route.

I had my answer when I touched soft fabric on the next branch. An old scrunchy, judging by the slack elastic, hung in the bark. I pocketed it. The rest of the way down was as easy as I remembered, and I made it to my car without setting off anyone's alarm.

# CHAPTER 13

# JD: SUNDAY NIGHT, HOUSTON

Triumphant, but feeling ridiculous about it—what had I done besides avoid death, injury, or humiliating discovery?—I turned my attention to what to do next and where to stay the night. Dinner wouldn't be a bad idea either. I drove into the Village, the little shopping center that was so important to West University Place. These days, the threat of Generica and its big chain stores nipped at the Village's boundaries, but locally owned businesses still dominated. The Village had charm, everyone said. I wasn't sure charm would prevail, but so far people seemed glad to pay for Retail Disneyland, with boutiques, faux vintage establishments, unique restaurants, and specialty shops of every kind.

I ordered a pastrami-on-rye sandwich at Alfred's Deli. My mother and I used to go there. She always took her kids out for special occasions. After the twins were born, she made sure that she and I had our own private time, often at Alfred's.

I went back whenever I was in Houston, and if I squinched my eyes, I could imagine Mother sitting across from me, asking about my day, and would I please ask Alfred to wrap up a half-pound of smoked gouda, a pound of corned beef, and some of those little candies the twins liked. I didn't want to tell her that one of her precious girls was lost, that I couldn't find Merry anywhere. At the same time, something like a prayer for help rumbled in my brain.

Now that I had better light, I pulled the scrunchy out of my pocket to try to identify its owner. Red or pink would be Cherry; any shade of blue or lavender, Merry. Faded and torn, the ornament had started its life as a noncommittal green. I would have picked Cherry, the wild twin, for the climber, but Merry's actions over the last months proved she could escape when she felt like it.

Watching the young waitstaff, probably third-generation Alfreds, gave me an idea. After I finished my sandwich, I strolled down the street to The Sweet Shoppe, the twins' favorite place to go with Mother. Even on Sunday night, it was full of dating couples and families with small children. The waitstaff was mostly too young to help me, but I spotted a manager a few years my senior. I waited for a lull in her ice cream slinging and then approached.

"Hello, I—"

"JD Thompson! How are you doing? How are Merry and Cherry?"

Looking harder, I recognized our fluffy-haired waitress from long ago, the one who acted like it was a privilege to wait on the Thompson family, which it might have been, considering how my mother tipped. I captured the manager's name with a flying glance at her name tag. It's rude to stare at women's chests, but why do they put their ID there? "Alexandra Adamson" meant nothing to me, but then my brain gave a grudging click.

"Sandy!" I exclaimed as my memory flashed the image of her former saucer-sized, bowed-and-beribboned name tag. "I never knew you were related to the owners."

She'd abandoned the poodle-style curls of her youth. Her hair now curled into a sleek dark knot at her neck, and she'd replaced her makeup with subtle shades instead of slabs of whitewash on her cheeks and color around her eyes. I called that style *raccoon corpse*. I liked the current Sandy, that is, Alexandra, better. I took another strafing glance at her left hand as she worked on her next treat. Sadly, she wore a nice set of rings.

She said between scoops and squirts, "My parents made sure I knew the business from the ground up—and no special favors for me. They're now enjoying the beach in Florida, and I'm keeping the doors open here."

"Looks like you're doing well." The number of patrons and the well-maintained furnishings told me that.

"It's a different world today, harder for a mom-and-pop store. I'd be happy to sell, if I could find a buyer who'd pay decently." She laughed again. "The expression on your face! That's how all my old customers look—'No, you can't possibly!' But how often do you come in?"

I laughed too. "Be fair—I don't live in Houston, and this was my sisters' special spot."

Sandy waved over one of her staff to handle the register. With the tall drink she prepared in one hand, she grabbed a bottle of water with the other before coming around the counter to join me. She gestured to a table in the corner, so close to the window and the serving counter that no one would choose it except as a last resort.

She handed me the drink. "Chocolate shake, right?"

"Um, yes. You remember all your old customers' orders?" My diet no longer included frequent chocolate shakes, but I wasn't going to refuse it. After the first sip, I had to blink back the sudden moisture in my eyes as my traitorous memory dumped out a flood of recollections—sights, sounds, smells, tastes.

"Not all, but lots. I have to work harder to remember their names, but I can't go around yelling, 'Hey, Chocolate Shake? How's Strawberry Soda and Double-Scoop Peppermint?'"

Remembering Cherry's order earlier in the day, I laughed with her. "Have you seen them lately? They've been in and out of Houston all summer, and I was hoping to run into them. Their twenty-first birthday is coming up soon, and we need to make plans, if they'd ever stay still long enough." I craned my neck to look around the store. "Do you still have a party room? Maybe we could have it here."

Sadness flickered across her face. "Oh, JD, after your mother passed, they never enjoyed this place. You and your grandmother were good about bringing them here for all their occasions, but they always looked ready to cry." Her chuckle sounded watery. "I'd give them extra cherries and bigger scoops of ice cream with more sprinkles. That's when I learned that extra sugar doesn't cure everything, practically a heresy in my family."

I swallowed over the lump in my throat. "If no one ever said it, I appreciate your trying. It was a tough time for all of us." I remembered dragging the twins here, determined to make things as they used to be, which they never could be again. It was for me as much as for them and worked just as well.

"I understand. Your mother was a special lady." Alexandra shook her head. "I haven't seen the twins in ages. I'd see them from time to time in high school—they were Village Girls instead of Mall Rats, but they usually didn't come in." Her smile managed a return appearance. "Most kids want alcohol at their twenty-first birthday parties. You'll need another location for that."

"Even so, I bet they'd like an ice cream cake or one of your other specialties. I'll mention it—if I ever catch up to them. If you see them wandering about, tell them to call me. Kids today! Never check their messages on any platform. Am I right?" A few more gulps finished my shake, and a few more pleasantries ended the visit.

Feeling chased by ghosts from the past, I jumped into my car and sped south for Galveston, like it would be any less haunted. I contrasted my frequent returns to Alfred's Deli because it reminded me of Mother, to the twins' avoidance of The Sweet Shoppe because it reminded them of Mother. Someday when I was feeling generous, I might revisit my opinions about the shrouded portraits in Dad's closet.

It was after ten when I checked into the Hotel Galvez, where we'd stayed on our last family vacation. I rented a suite, the only space available during these last days of summer vacation and the beginning of fall renovations. That served me right for making no plans at all. On my phone, I found a business week special, five-nights-for-three. I winced as the bored desk clerk swiped my card. I'd be eating ramen noodles for the next quarter.

# CHAPTER 14
# JD: MONDAY THROUGH WEDNESDAY, GALVESTON

ow many times have I awakened in the Galveston area with sun streaming in through a slit in the curtains? All those times, the joyous feeling of "Vacation!" pounded through my veins, especially on the first day. The long lazy days stretched ahead to forever, and wonderful things could happen.

This time, the sun still streamed in through the curtains, because the only way to keep out Texas sun is with a plywood panel caulked around the edges. But I groaned as I achieved consciousness from disrupted sleep. All I could remember of the dream was my mother's voice saying over and over, with the barest edge of desperation, "JD, would you look after the twins?"

For days I'd spent the morning liminal space, that uncertain time between rolling out of bed and coffee, telling myself that I was an adult, the twins were adults, I could not have prevented anything that happened to them or that they chose to do, and I was not responsible for anybody but myself. Today I said, "Sure, Mother," and kicked my butt in gear.

Armed with laptop and phone, I set up office at the breakfast buffet to coordinate all the info Cherry finally got around to sending about their childhood friends, anybody that Merry might have turned to. I shouldn't have been surprised at how many names there were. The cute blonde twins had been active and popular in school and church. Also, Cherry had reached hard, long, and deep into her contacts list—basically everybody she'd ever met.

I mentally shook myself and looked out the restaurant window at the expanse of sand and water. A perfect place for Merry. I'd taken them for so many walks on the beach to gather shells and other beach whatnot. Cherry treated the outings like an Easter egg hunt, to see how much she could gather in the least amount of time. Merry stopped to study each item she picked up and ask me impossible questions about it.

Phones weren't nearly the source of information they are now—mine wasn't, anyway—so we'd spend hours on the laptop back in the hotel room looking up beach creatures and their detritus until Cherry demanded that we play a game, watch a movie, anything else at all. I'd take them out for one last shrieking run around the cottage before bedtime to make sure they'd fall asleep right away.

I slammed the door on memories and returned to my freshly cleaned suite. I searched for these so-called friends on multiple devices, multiple apps, even the occasional phone call. Room service brought me lunch. I alternated between Cokes, water, coffee, and tea until I had to clear off my table-cum-desk just to use my equipment.

I don't know which was more frustrating: people who didn't respond immediately to an elder brother planning his sisters' birthday party or people who wanted to catch up and chat forever, like Heather Webster. She called right after I texted her because it had been an age since she'd seen me, did I know all the twins' friends had huge crushes on me, and how were they anyway.

Something inside me snapped. "Cherry was okay when I saw her last weekend. I haven't seen Merry for months." I tried to regroup. "She went off on her own this summer. I heard she'd been in Houston, off and on, so I came to talk to her about the party. Have you run into her?"

"No, but I'm in Texas City now, so I don't see my Houston friends as much as I'd like."

I didn't tell her that I was only fourteen miles away from her. A little bit of Heather went a long way.

I thought I might have a better chance of reaching people in the evening. So I set out to visit our old vacation spots and search for possible workplaces. If Merry decided to stay in the Galveston area, she'd need a job, and a tourist resort always has plenty of crummy jobs.

*Decided*. That word assumed she could decide anything. I clung to that desperate hope.

A little bit of Galveston went a long way too. I'm not sure I ever saw a resident. The cost of living was too high for the average wage-earner, and the crowds I pushed through were eking out the last bit of summer joy before school-year drudgery reclaimed them.

I showed my sister's photo to workers and random people who looked like residents, with cover stories. (1) My sister works here—I think she said it was here. (2) I was supposed to meet my sister here for lunch; has she showed up? (3) I'm assistant justice of the peace for Alvarez County (flashing the card Johnny printed for me, because I'm his unpaid assistant), working on Case #WH1cH3V34 (all true, though assistant justices of the peace don't go around investigating police cases).

I even showed her photo to some big sea monster in the aquarium. We were on eye level, and his expression made me feel like we might have communicated, at least as well as I was doing with Merry's friends, if only water and species hadn't kept us apart.

Thus was my grind from day to day. On Tuesday I placed a hesitant call to the church where Mother and then Grandmother took us every Sunday. I discovered that my last youth minister was the twins' first and was now one of the church's associate pastors. Somehow neither my birthday spiel nor my investigator act seemed appropriate. After confirming confidentiality—like lawyers, clergy can keep secrets unless a crime is involved—I told her the bald truth. She'd helped guide the twins after Mother died, and she promised to do what she could to find anyone who might have been close enough for Merry to turn to.

"And how are you doing?" she asked.

I hadn't had much to do with the church after Mother died. My being away at college was less of a reason than God's failure to answer the one prayer of my teenage years.

That was a good conversation, with shreds of sorrow.

On Wednesday Grandfather called, wanting to know what was wrong with my father, why he wasn't pulling out all stops for a full investigation.

"You're asking me?" I demanded. "When have I ever understood what he does?"

"I thought he might have told you."

"He just told me to mind my own business, that finding my sister wasn't it."

His voice sounded as soothing as dark honey. "Parents frequently look on their children as children, even when the child is almost thirty."

"It's more a question of looking on me as an idiot."

"I would phrase it that he doesn't understand your choices. You're doing good work in your community, but he'd prefer seeing you on a more traditional career path."

I traipsed around the room like an animal in a cage. "Right, either working toward a judgeship or rising to a partnership in corporate law. I tried both, and the pace felt like treading water in amber."

"You never made peace with the way the legal world works."

"No, I didn't," I said, my voice rising up into Dianne's range. "In grammar school, I learned that someone might shoot up my school. Remember Columbine? Then came 9/11 to teach me that someone could fly a plane into my office. A certain lack of honesty surrounded that event, and I lost a friend in the war that followed. And any nut job can still lay classrooms full of kids to waste in less than five minutes—sorry, Dad's straight and narrow path holds no appeal. If I'm going to do anything with my life, I'd better do it now. Like the space princess said, 'Instant gratification takes too long' when any moment could be your last."

The grandfather clock in his living room chimed. He sounded more thoughtful when he spoke again. "Hmm. When I was young, I saw the president assassinated on TV—in Texas, no less. A few years later, somebody climbed to the top of the University of Texas clock tower and shot almost fifty people before the police took him down. I confess that's the first thing I thought of when you wanted to attend UT. A few years later, the National Guard shot and killed four students at Kent State. I don't say these were the same as your experiences, but I responded differently."

"Right. Enlisting in the Marines. Not something I'd do," I agreed. "I mean, thank you for your service. I wonder what Dad's generation-breaking events were."

His voice rumbled with amusement, sounding more polite than appreciative. "He's never mentioned them. Of course, you didn't either. We often thought the children wouldn't notice."

I snorted. "Him, maybe. The rest of us, yeah, we did."

"I do appreciate what you're doing now."

I ground my teeth. "But a police department could be doing it better, since it's like looking for a seven-year-old's flip-flops on Galveston beach. Ask me how I know. I thought I'd have an advantage, with my 'special knowledge' of my sister. That does not appear to be the case. I might have better luck dredging the bayou by our old house."

"What?"

I flinched at the horror in his voice. I'd shocked myself too. I rubbed the aching spot between my eyes. "I've no idea where that came from. Forget it. I'm worn out."

That was a bad conversation.

I soon learned from the dirty looks and helpful offerings from the hotel restaurant staff that lingering over a meal wasn't appreciated. Room service on the regular would bankrupt me, but I also learned that the bar would bring me a burger, and no one would disturb me if I had a drink in front of me, neither servers nor hopeful women. Or men.

In keeping with the historic nature and decor of the hotel, the wood-paneled bar was a hushed venue, like a meditation retreat, instead of a place to party down at the top of your lungs to the depths of your stomach. I sought solace in the darkest corner each night, where I allowed myself twenty minutes of not checking my messages. Utter loneliness always set in, and I longed for Gregg House, always popu-lated, never crowded, with always a listening ear, either sympathetic, tough-love, or both.

I'd reached that maudlin state when Dianne blazed up to my table, her eyes flashing fire like her Mexican warrior ancestors.

"I should have known I'd find you here! You deserve to be sacrificed to Quetzalcoatl."

I don't say I saw flames from her mouth like her ancestral deity, but I don't deny it either.

# CHAPTER 15

# JD: WEDNESDAY NIGHT, GALVESTON

I couldn't imagine why she was so upset. I couldn't imagine how she found me either, but I was glad to see her, even in full Quetzal mode.

I picked up my drink and held it out to her. "Have a seat. You want this?"

"You've got some nerve!"

I frowned, trying to identify my sin. The bartender called to her, "Let me make you another, Miss. He's been staring that one down to water all evening. Same thing?"

"What? No, thank you. I'm driving. JD, why do you have a drink if you're not drinking it?"

"Because then people leave me alone. What are you doing here?"

"Everyone was worried about you. You haven't sent more than an emoji or single words since you set out. I thought I knew the answer when I found you holed up in a bar." She scorched me again with her gaze.

"Do I need to swear on my mother's wedding portrait that I'm not drinking?" My throat thickened shut. I had a hard time getting words out. "I've lost my mother. I may have lost my sister. But I am not losing ... my home. I'll do the next Dry January to prove it."

"You didn't get falling down drunk after your mother died."

"I didn't want to kill my feelings. I wanted to hurt for the rest of my life." I stared beyond the paneled walls into the past. "I got better, somewhat."

Dianne clutched her arms across her chest. "JD, I'm going to take a brisk walk outside around the hotel. When I come back, we will start this conversation over."

I started to stand up. "Let me go with you, at least behind you. You could run in to anybody walking outside alone at night in a resort."

She planted a hand on my shoulder and shoved me back into the booth, harder than necessary. "I hope I do. I'd be thrilled for the chance to cut someone's liver out."

As the server set another glass of water in front of me, he said with the faintest leer, "Don't have to worry about her. *She* can take care of herself."

"I'm more worried about who she meets. As her attorney, it gets harder to explain the trail of broken bodies."

Having no response to that, he crept away, and I savored the water like it had a taste and bouquet. I placed it as Galveston tap water from around 4:00 p.m., needing a few more runs through the filter to reach its prime and banish the hint of chlorine and chewiness.

Dianne floated in, closer to her serene self than previously, two-thirds of the way down the glass, thus sparing me a trip outside to look for her when the glass was empty.

"So, did you meet any pendejos?"

"No, qué lástima. But we are starting this conversation over, now that I've walked off my rage. My friend's therapist says it takes ninety seconds for an emotion to dissipate."

"Funny, I thought group therapy was something different."

"Nobody can afford all the therapy they need. So we share. Now, are we starting over?"

"Dianne! What a nice surprise. Why are you here? How did you find me?"

Her special flirtatious smile slunk across her face, even more toasty than usual from the exercise. "Oh, I couldn't stay away. Do you want the whole story?"

"Of course I do."

# CHAPTER 16
# DIANNE: SUNDAY
# THROUGH MONDAY, BEAUCHAMP

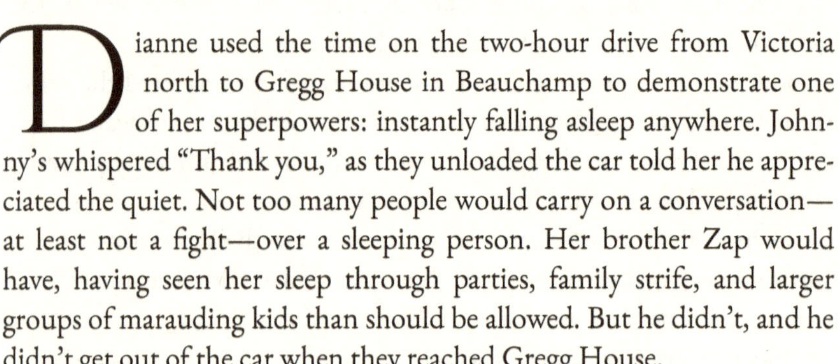

Dianne used the time on the two-hour drive from Victoria north to Gregg House in Beauchamp to demonstrate one of her superpowers: instantly falling asleep anywhere. Johnny's whispered "Thank you," as they unloaded the car told her he appreciated the quiet. Not too many people would carry on a conversation—at least not a fight—over a sleeping person. Her brother Zap would have, having seen her sleep through parties, family strife, and larger groups of marauding kids than should be allowed. But he didn't, and he didn't get out of the car when they reached Gregg House.

Dianne tapped the driver's window. "You don't have to go back right away. Come in and have dinner first."

Zap glanced at Johnny, climbing the steps to the back porch. "What are you having? Boiled grass and berries?"

Dianne almost succeeded in not smiling. "Johnny will be fixing something vegetarian, yes, but I have a bag of bacon in the freezer. Chicken tinga too. So you're not taking Cherry back to Waco?"

He scowled at Cherry as she bumped her suitcase up the back porch steps. "No. She's *sure* her boss will understand if she calls in tonight. But as for me staying—do you think you'll hear anything from JD? If there's a chance of that—No, I can't sit across from her anymore. What was she thinking? Merry might be dead because of her!"

Dianne lowered her voice as he raised his. "And she feels that now. I agree, she's pulled one stupid stunt, even though she thought she was protecting her sister. I don't expect to hear from JD so soon—he just arrived in Houston—but if I do, I'll let you know."

He nodded as he shifted the car to reverse. "Thanks. If I leave now, I can get to Austin before all the restaurants close. I'd rather have barbecue ribs from LeRoy and Lewis than Johnny's yard clippings."

After waving goodbye and entering the house, Dianne dropped her bag by the stairs and joined everyone in the kitchen. Darryl bustled around the kitchen as Johnny's assistant. Looking uncertain, Cherry sat at the table and watched them. Johnny was charring peppers, multiple kinds in happy colors, one on each grill over the gas burner. Dianne asked him, "Anything I can do?"

Johnny tried to point to the kitchen island with his shoulder as he turned each pepper over in quick succession. He was trying to turn the skin black, not burn it to an unusable crisp. "I laid out something for you."

Dianne suppressed a smile as she took in the recipe, the small chopping board, and the ingredients, including spices. Her practice of random substitutions horrified Johnny, and he always gathered the ingredients and laid out the recipe for her.

She'd honed her own cooking skills while caring for younger siblings and cousins. When small voices howled in hunger, she threw together meals as fast as she could, substituting or dropping ingredients at will. The family still laughed about the time she tried to fulfill a birthday child's request for macaroni and cheese by covering her aunt's gourmet farfalle with brie, bleu cheese, and a nice, aged sharp cheddar with port wine. When the children declared it gross, not anything like mac and cheese from a box, she ordered a pizza and charged it to her aunt. The grownups loved the dish, and now someone always brought a batch to family parties.

"Do you want to help me?" Dianne asked Cherry. Maybe they could talk.

Cherry edged away from the kitchen into the gallery hall. "I should call my boss."

"You haven't already?" asked Dianne, feigning surprise.

"Um, no. I didn't wanna wake you in the car. I'll be back in a few."

She reappeared fifteen minutes later with red and swollen eyes. "They said I could take off as much time as I needed. Do you still need help with dinner?"

"Everything is in progress." Johnny's voice was barely audible over the clanging pots.

"And I just finished setting the table," said Darryl, as he placed the last napkin and patted it. "But you could take care of Godzilla."

"That weird cat you got at Christmas? The hairless one that looks like a plucked chicken?" Cherry wrinkled her nose in disgust. "The one that sent you to the emergency room?"

"That's the one," Darryl confirmed. "Our little demon Sphynx. He's a lot better, but he still doesn't like me. Let me show you how to take care of him. He's hungry."

"What makes you think he'll like me?" Cherry's voice rose in alarm.

"He doesn't like dudes," Darryl called over his shoulder as he led the way to Godzilla's lair. "Like I said, he's getting better. You'll be fine. In fact, I think he's hiding out in your bedroom, the one downstairs on the right, correct? You guys can bond."

Darryl was a force not to be resisted, but Cherry looked terrified.

"You're perfectly safe with him," Dianne called after them. "He never attacks me. Tomorrow Chantal will be back, and he's technically her cat. When she's on the road, he stays with us. Mostly he hides."

"Under the bed," affirmed Darryl. "I've hardly seen him all weekend. The way I like it."

Cherry survived her acquaintance with Godzilla, but she insisted that he not spend the night in her room.

The next morning Dianne did yoga at dawn with Johnny. After they walked at a brisk pace through Beauchamp, Dianne felt so restored to her routine that she did a happy Kizomba dance into her office.

She found Chantal seated in one of the client chairs, her laptop already open. Pink-skinned Godzilla furrowed his multileveled brow and glared at Dianne from his perch on the desk, just to make his point, whatever that was. Dianne still thought he was the ugliest cat ever, created on a day God called in sick, but she was proud she didn't flinch at the sight of him anymore. For contrast, she scratched the golden ears of the most beautiful cat in the world, her own Nevada, snuggled down in a peach plush bed by the monitor.

Knowing her friend spent the previous night singing in Dallas, Dianne said to Chantal, "You're up early."

Snuggling her cheek against Godzilla's until he turned around and thrust his tail in her face, Chantal mumbled, "I need a new speaker, so I'll take all the work you can give me. Bound to be some small businesses turning their stuff in. I don't have any gigs until next weekend."

Dianne smiled. Her fingers flew across the keyboard as she dumped digital files into Chantal's work folder. Out of the corner of her eye, Dianne saw emails flooding the company inbox. She'd sent out an email the previous week to remind their business partnership and S-corporation clients to turn in their numbers by August 15 if they wanted Black Orchid Enterprises to complete their taxes by September 15, the final date for these entities to file the previous year's taxes.

From his desk by the front door, Darryl was calling to remind the clients who hadn't responded. "This is Darryl Swann with Black Orchid Enterprises, just calling to remind you to turn in your records by August 15, or we can't guarantee we'll have them done on time." He paused to listen. "Yes, sir, you can bring in your paper records, if you get them here by August 15."

Dianne and Chantal groaned.

Darryl dialed and repeated his previous message. After another listening pause, he said, "I'm sorry, Ms. Cortez is unavailable." He continued in a different voice, "Same to you, hog breath. How rude!"

Nevada raised her head in alarm. Dianne stroked her head and murmured comfort, trusting that Darryl was shouting to empty air.

Chantal asked, "I thought I saw one of JD's sisters here. I've always seen them as a matched set. Is this one the one who was missing?"

Sighing again, Dianne stroked her cat, who might have stuck her tongue out at Godzilla. "No, she's still missing. You haven't heard the latest."

"Dish, girl."

Dianne did.

Sometime later, Chantal shook her head. "Those Thompsons. Johnny puts out more effort to find a lost cat. Any other white family would have their missing girl on the six o'clock news. Missing blonde girls are hot stuff. How's JD taking it?"

"You know JD."

"I certainly do. That's why I ask."

Dianne handed her phone to Chantal with JD's recent texts showing. "When we left him on Sunday, on his way to single-handedly find his sister in their childhood environs, he looked noble and brave."

"Probably a quivering mass of goo by now."

Dianne agreed. "That, or a river rock. JD folds up inside when things get bad. That's when ..."

"When what?"

Torn by loyalty, Dianne decided that secrets just caused suffering, as recent events proved. "When he drinks."

"JD doesn't drink. Not badly. You want to see people drink, come look at my family. Of course, in New Orleans, there's four bars on every street corner, to help you along to alcoholic heaven, but there's no law that says you have to visit them every day, whatever my Uncle Andre says."

"I can look at my own family. You mostly see JD on stage. He doesn't drink then."

"He tried once, back in college, but I told him, 'You can drink, or you can perform, but not both, not in my band.' He never took another drop, not till the lights went out afterwards. And not even then, when he was driving. He'd just watched the wrong movies about the wild life of musicians. They're not documentaries."

"It's not a question of drinking the bars dry. It's more like drinking is his solution to hard problems. After two nights of watching him drink himself insensible, I told him if he ever did it again, Johnny and I were throwing him out of the house."

"You didn't!

"I did!" Dianne hated how her voice sounded like a sob. "And now —when I took his little sister away so he could search without her falling to pieces—"

"Saint Guadalupe Dianne, Martyr."

"What if I just made it possible for him to drink himself sick?"

"Dianne, he is a grown-ass man. He can choose which handbasket he wants to go to hell in."

Dianne folded her arms and rested her forehead on them. "I just, I just don't want to help pick the color."

"Dianne, they used to say at those meetings we went to for Uncle Andre, there's nothing you can do to make him stop drinking, and nothing you can do to make him start. You got to get over this. Unless you had Spec's Liquor deliver a case of bourbon to his room, then you might feel a little bad about it." Chantal did a fist pump as she finished another return.

Dianne answered with a fist bump. "Of course I didn't. I don't even know where he is. It's just ..."

"It would be easier if you didn't love him."

"It would," Dianne whispered.

# CHAPTER 17

# DIANNE: MONDAY THROUGH WEDNESDAY, BEAUCHAMP

Dianne focused on her monitor to avoid Chantal's eyebrows, rising slowly. "Just leave it, okay? I'm not up for another conversation about the different kinds of love. I've never denied I love JD in some way."

"You must have forgotten—"

"If I have, I don't want to be reminded."

In the dead silence, Cherry stomped into the office and flopped onto one of the sleek, spindly metal client chairs, quite a feat with furniture designed to keep people from hanging around.

In accusing tones, she announced, "Johnny said I'd be taking care of the cats, and all I've done is scoop litter boxes. Is there anything else I could do?"

In the time it took for Dianne to sigh from the top of her head to her toes—her version of counting to ten—the phone rang twice. Dianne asked, "Cherry, could you answer the phones?"

Cherry brightened. "Of course I can! I answer the phone all the time at my job."

Chantal yawned again. "Ever thought of an auto-answer? Didn't we use one in April?"

"Yes, but the only people not filling out tax forms then were the cats. It's part of our brand, to have our clients reach a person quickly. We offer personal attention, worth paying extra, unlike faceless corporations do."

Darryl answered another call. "Black Orchid Enterprises. I'm sorry, we can't guarantee to have your taxes filed on time if you don't have your records to us by August 15." After a moment, he shouted in answer to Dianne, "Yeah, give them the chance to yell at someone right away. Same to you sideways with hot sauce, buddy."

"Darryl," warned Dianne as she pushed back her chair.

"I know, I know. What if a client walked in the front door just then, yada etc. yada," he groused.

Dianne beckoned Cherry to Darryl's desk. "Darryl, Cherry's going to answer the phones. That should help your productivity."

"Yeah, 'cause when I finish the file I opened thirty minutes ago, I'll have one done for the morning."

Dianne persevered. "Show her how the different lines work: Legal, Accounting, Vet and Animal Control, Justice of the Peace. Take her through the scripts."

Cherry grew cheerful. "I can do that. I'm an actress."

Darryl demanded, "Did you change all the litter boxes in the shelter already? The clinic too? What about their food? I fixed the special diet bowls for you."

"No, I wanted to ask Dianne—"

"We don't do that, leave the cats hungry, sitting in their crates with nothing to eat but their own poop. How'd you like to be trapped in a bathroom with a full toilet?"

"Does anybody in this house ever think of anything but cats?" shrieked Cherry.

"Any reason to?" called Chantal from Dianne's office. "By the way, you're upsetting my cat. It's all right, sweetums. They're not going to hurt you. I won't let them, and Johnny will go all Bruce Lee on them if they try. Yes, he will."

Dianne said in measured but definite tones developed in her years as the oldest child in a large family. "Cherry will carry the phone with her as she completes those vital duties. The sooner you teach her the scripts, the sooner she can finish tending the cats. Oh, and Cherry? Darryl is the boss of you in these essential office functions."

Darryl and Cherry glared at each other. He gestured to one of the client chairs by the door as the phone rang. "Pull up a chair and take notes, Cherry. Black Orchid Enterprises, Accounting."

Dianne waited long enough to confirm that all insurrections were quelled. She returned to her office to find Nevada and Godzilla squaring off, Nevada in her bed, Godzilla draped over Chantal's arm as she brought her laptop to life.

"Don't you guys start," muttered Dianne in a reverse stage whisper, the kind that only the people on stage with you can hear. "I did not sign up to run a preschool."

Chantal snuggled her cheek against her cat's face. "There now, Zil. Nevada's your friend."

The cats hissed one last time before settling down to pretend no other cat ever existed.

Silence reigned while the three humans ground out return after return, Dianne and Chantal taking the complex ones for businesses, Darryl the simple ones for individuals who weren't waiting for the October 15 final deadline. He claimed the forms read, "How much money did you make? Send it," which wasn't far wrong.

Chantal's presence added a layer of worry for Johnny at mealtimes. Not because of her diabetic needs—he'd dealt with those for years. She embraced a free-wheeling style towards recipes—like Dianne, she threw in whatever was handy as opposed to what was listed. But Johnny considered her attitude towards spices worse. Claiming that White people's spices from the grocery store were mostly shredded cardboard, she tripled all spice requirements. If she was missing one spice, she'd add more of the others to make up.

Dianne agreed with her about grocery store spices, but she knew Johnny bought or grew the best, most intense spices, and she had enough respect for that fact and for numbers in general not to improvise the amounts. So Johnny set out their recipes and ingredients, and Dianne did her best to keep Chantal within recipe limits and to separate Darryl and Cherry, who continued sniping at each other. Dianne recalled the ten housemates she'd had in college and wondered how they all made it through—and were still friends, some of them still living together. She grudgingly gave JD some credit for his chill, laid-back personality that could calm most troubled waters.

By Wednesday, Dianne thought they could plow through the remaining returns without even working until midnight, removing at least one stressor. That afternoon, however, the Denton family blew in through the front door and yelled for Johnny.

Mr. Denton bellowed, "We've been calling all morning, and nobody answered. Do you people run a business here?"

Cherry had just returned to the front desk from the cat shelter in Darryl's absence, since he was assisting Johnny in the clinic. She fetched the phone from her scrub top and grimaced in alarm. She punched buttons, and the phone chirped back to life. Dianne pressed the intercom to summon Johnny before joining the Dentons in the hall. Chantal shook her head and kept working.

Dianne pulled herself up to her full height, intimidating in itself, she'd been told, and asked in her chilliest voice, "May I help you?"

"That little Asian guy put Avabella in the database against our will!" yelled the man.

"I'm sure he didn't." Dianne had no idea what they were talking about. She was relieved to see Johnny emerge from the clinic. He still wore his blood-stained surgical scrubs, it being community spay-neuter day, but that sight repelled the guests only for a moment.

"You gave Avabella that DNA kit, and now the government's gonna know all about her genes," Mr. Denton shouted.

"No, I did not. I tried to give it to your wife, but she turned away. When Avabella took it, I assumed of course that she'd give it to your wife, that your wife knew she had it."

Mrs. Denton gasped. "Well, I never! I did not want it. She hid it from me and sent it in herself. I just got an email from them saying that the results would be ready any day, since they were for an open criminal case. You have to stop them!"

Johnny's hands shook. "I do not know how I could or why you would want it done. Avabella's DNA would be the best match with her mother's, and you said you wanted to locate your sister, to determine whether the recently discovered bones were hers."

"And I told you we didn't want any DNA testing," insisted Mr. Denton. "Who knows what the government would do with it?"

"I told you too," echoed his wife, with a glare at Johnny.

Dianne's voice went even more gelid. "We will discuss the matter with our attorney and take his advice."

Johnny's expression stayed blank, though his hands still shook. "I'll see if I can get in touch with them, but they've probably already run the tests."

Dianne moved forward. "We'll keep you advised."

They hadn't much choice but to back up in face of her cold force. She slammed and locked the front door behind them. She turned around to lean against the door. "We need JD, but I don't even know how to find him."

"Of course you do," said Johnny.

# CHAPTER 18

# JD: WEDNESDAY NIGHT, GALVESTON

I sat upright so fast I knocked over my glass of water. I grabbed it before all of it spilled. "Johnny put tracking devices on all our cars? Does he subscribe to the Detective Gadget of the Month Club?"

"I don't think it's that formal, but he does read all the literature and orders anything that looks interesting. You knew about this. You were there when we discussed it."

"Sometimes you guys just witter away like birds. You rip your topic into the tiniest pieces, down to the molecules, and, yeah, sometimes I check out."

"Oh. I always thought you were writing poetry in some kind of fugue state. You were just bored." Disappointment infused Dianne's words.

"I try to listen hard enough in case you decide I should replace the roof on the house."

"Could you?"

"No! That's why I half-listen."

"I don't think it needs replacing now. Johnny's grandmother had all the maintenance likely for the near future done when she remodeled the house to include his vet clinic. But it would be good to know whether you can."

"No! I can't climb on the top story and wave around huge sheets of metal in the gale-force winds Texas calls a light breeze."

"Really? You used to do a lot of the maintenance on that house we rented in college."

"None of which included the roof, only emergency repairs like broken windows. I am so over that. Growing up means paying other people for your life maintenance."

"Does it? Seems like a waste of money that you could put toward retirement if you have the proper skills, which you should acquire if you don't have them."

"We're wandering from why all our vehicles have tracking devices."

"JD, it's not that big of a thing. Some of my tíos put them on their teenagers' cars. And that emergency phone app you and Johnny made for everyone in Casa Cortez after Lisa died wasn't exactly a tracker, but it gave the caller's location so someone could come help."

I remembered my phone shouting ABBA's "SOS" and me telling my date I had to go because my housemate was in trouble. Sometimes that didn't go over well. "Different. You were in control. You decided when you were unsafe and needed someone to know your location."

"Think of it as a backup for when you don't know if you're safe or when you can't make the notification yourself. Johnny and I started talking about it because he drives all over the desolate parts of the county either on justice of the peace or substitute vet calls. And Chantal drives by herself to these dives she calls music venues, all over the state, usually in the middle of the night. You can take the tracker off your car if you want, but think of all the driving you do, back and forth to the border towns to immigration court. And it brought me to you tonight." In a different tone, she whispered, "I was worried about you. You just sent emoji and one-word texts."

I thought I understood. "Oh—like Cherry did, pretending to be Merry. I can see how your mind would go there, but you knew I was safe, that it was me, typing on my own phone. I just didn't want to talk about my complete lack of progress with only my fears for company. Each day brought me closer to the hopelessness of it all, that my sister's gone forever. I just couldn't talk about it."

"That's what I thought. That things were so bad you couldn't talk." Even with a lull in the usual barroom noise, I could barely hear her.

We looked into each other's eyes in smoldering silence. She grabbed her purse and stood up. "If I'm getting back to Beauchamp tonight, I'd better get on the road."

I glanced out the window into the darkness. "Why would you go now? It'll take you over three hours to get home, and then you'll be wrecked the next day when you have to work."

"JD, I—"

After ten-ish years, we don't need many words to communicate, but all anyone would see was two silent people not quite looking at each other. The more perceptive ones might think that these people have a history that they're about to renew. I wanted that, against all reason, but I knew it was the worst idea for both of us. Dianne looked like she knew it too. Her lower lip moved the barest bit as she nipped its inner edge, her tell for desires at war. I'd never seen anything so sexy in all my life—I knew then I was lost.

I interrupted our broadcasting thoughts with one last noble effort. "I have a suite. You could have your own room."

Dianne's face bloomed into joy. "That's wonderful! But why do you have a suite?"

"Because I didn't reserve ahead of time, and that was all that was left. Now I'm glad." I stood up and threw money on the table for the staff. I try to tip in cash because too many establishments skim the employees' tips from credit card purchases.

"You have that kind of money?" She looked around at all the extra touches that claimed to be worth the bill I'd be presented with. She threw another ten-dollar bill on the table.

"No, but my grandfather is contributing to the cause. He thinks somebody should be looking for Merry, and he's as hacked off at my father as I am." I answered Dianne's querying eyebrows. "Dad's angry that I opened a missing person case, and he doesn't want me searching for her. He says he'll take care of it, but he's not. I told Officer Al that the Houston police would be contacting them. They haven't. Dad has all kinds of contacts and could easily get someone to investigate privately, but is he? Wouldn't we have stumbled into them by now? Wouldn't they have talked to Cherry, at least?"

We strolled to the elevator. Dianne pushed the Up button. "Maybe Cherry and Johnny will see them when they go to Waco tomorrow."

After we captured an elevator, I punched the top floor button and leaned against the car's wall. Dianne pressed into the opposite corner, as though to get as far away from me as possible. She would be happy to explain that the diagonal is a longer distance than straight across a square. Maybe she had a point, remembering all the elevators, closets, and temporarily unoccupied spaces where we used to—never mind. That was then. I tried to distract myself. "*Johnny* and Cherry are going to Waco, you said."

"He thinks there's more in Waco than we—or Cherry—know. He plans to talk to Merry's friends, the ones she doesn't share with Cherry. Cherry was combing Merry's social accounts for names when I left."

"Hmm." My mind boggled, trying to imagine Johnny volunteering for social occasions like talking to strangers. Of course, it was a case, a puzzle, which made it different. But still ...

Both our phones squawked in harmony with the elevator chime as we arrived at our floor.

"It's Cherry," said Dianne. "Blasting to all the hermanas y primas."

"And me. Dad wants to pull her out of her school and send her to the University of Houston while she lives in his house for her last year of college."

"Really, JD, is there any situation he doesn't make worse? Maybe it's better when he does neglect his children." Dianne's thumbs flew across her phone.

"Haven't found such a situation yet. I'll tell her I don't think it's even possible to transfer that quickly, and she should do anything he asks molto adagio, as slow as possible—or slower."

Our phone activity gave us a chance to pause.

Confronted with hotel halls, she and I have always danced our way to the door, even when not romantically involved. But her vibes shouted "Don't touch me!" which made me sad, although I understood. So I started a merengue, a sideways step and slide, not a challenge for either of us. Also, it didn't have to be a partner dance. I hummed "Tu Sonrisa" as I started the step-slide pattern. She joined in, across from me, but closer to the wall. That gave her more space to improvise with turns and skips.

Her smile crept out as we approached the suite's door. Dancing always makes her happy. Me too, especially dancing with her.

# CHAPTER 19

# JD: THURSDAY, GALVESTON

I lay awake for some time in hopes she'd change her mind. Getting back together under these circumstances wouldn't end well. But I'd welcome the distraction.

But neither she nor anyone else distracted me. I slept soundly until the morning sun streamed in, when I woke with a deep sigh. After making myself presentable—friendly yet with some authority was my goal—I went into the living room area. Dianne perched on the couch with her legs folded underneath, all her attention on her laptop. She waved a hand at coffee and continental breakfast.

I doctored my coffee. "Are you going back this morning?"

"I can, if I'm in your way." The keys clicked, never missing a beat.

"Not at all. I planned on being out for most of the day. But aren't you working on taxes?"

"I have my work. I can reach Chantal or Darryl if I need them." She held up her laptop, with Quetzalcoatl glowering at me. She lowered her gaze. "I'd rather keep working and avoid the downtime of driving, but I can leave if you'd rather."

"Whatever you—" I cut myself off in mid-platitude. "I like having you here. It's been lonely. I have a five-nights-for-three coupon, so I was going to leave tomorrow, unless I get a hot lead."

"Okay." She swallowed. "I was worried about you, and after the chaos of the last few days, I'd like to relax."

"I didn't have a chance to say it out loud, but thanks for taking my sister in. I really did not know how to take care of her."

Dianne waved a hand again, this time dismissing me. I took the hint and left.

I'd already explored the nearby tourist attractions, the ones Cherry remembered. I'd had such high hopes for the aquarium. It seemed a natural for Merry. Maybe it was too public for her, so this day I crossed Galveston Bay and explored the islands and peninsula to the north and to the east. They weren't as tourist-packed as the city of Galveston itself.

Merry's high school friends continued their delayed responses to my earlier posts, and I struggled to maintain my different personas—clueless brother planning a birthday party, clueless brother meeting his sister, clueless man looking for a young woman for unstated but official reasons. One guy of Merry's age did a double-take when he saw her photo. My hopes soared for a second until he said, "Hey, she's really cute. I'll keep an eye out for her."

Some people say that there are millions of universes where everything imaginable happens. In one of them, I socked that kid in the mouth. Not this universe, though, and I felt so bad for my violent impulse that I bought lunch from his hot dog stand. I regretted it.

By three o'clock, I'd had enough. It being summer, many hours of light remained, but I'd run out of islands and patience. I returned to the hotel to find Dianne still pecking at her laptop.

"Any luck?" She looked up when I growled. "After I finished some tax returns, I checked the databases, and Meredith Arline Thompson doesn't show up employed anywhere. I checked as many variants of her name as I could think of. For LOLs, I checked Charity Adrienne Thompson too. At least once, Merry had her sister's ID."

"You let me wander up and down the islands in hundred-degree heat when you could access her employment info with a keystroke while sitting in the air conditioned inside?"

"I know people. And it was a few keystrokes." One shoulder lifted under her peach-colored tank top. She held up her fingers and counted. "Remember, there's a time lag, at least several weeks, on data posting.

Also, these are official, tax-withholding jobs. By the time you talk about contracting, subcontracting, freelancing, and just plain illegal—"

I frowned as I sank into the swoop-armed chair that must have cost the hotel at least thirty dollars at the Lumps R Us Warehouse. "We immigration lawyers say *undocumented*."

"When talking about employers who connive at, avoid, and downright break the law, *illegal* describes their activities perfectly."

I proclaimed and almost quoted from my high-school Shakespeare class, "So there are more things in the job market and employment, Horatio, than are dreamt of in your philosophy?"

"Please do not get poetical during business hours, JD." She pointed to another finger. "Another possibility is that Merry could have a new ID altogether. I checked for your mother's name, with no results, but beyond that, I'd no idea where to start."

I didn't either. Merry wouldn't have used the names of her book and movie heroines. She would know she couldn't get Leia O. Solo, Diana Prince, Katniss Everdeen, or Weetzie Bat past any HR department. One of my apps pinged to let me know that another of Merry's friends hadn't seen her in ages and would love to come to the party. I sank deeper into gloom and the chair.

Dianne noticed. "Tell you what, JD. I've found a new salsa place that's supposed to be great. It's on Highway 45, north of here in Dickinson, south of NASA. So not far. Let's go there. We've got the time and the tire rubber, and you need a break."

"Dianne, have you ever been anywhere for more than a day without finding the latest, greatest salsa club?"

"No. Why would I?"

"You can't suppress your superpower. What's its name?"

"Ojos Locos."

"Hang on." I called the friend who'd just contacted me. "Hey, Elisa. Thanks for the answer. I'll let you know the party details when I have them. Have to get the twins to sit down and plan first. Cherry's too busy and Merry's off somewhere enjoying the last days of vacay before the semester."

Some people think you can't hear eyeballs rolling, but I could hear Dianne's.

I exchanged more pleasantries with Elisa and continued my stealth attack. "My partner and I heard about this salsa club, Ojos Locos, south of NASA on Highway 45. Is it any good? It is? We'll give it a try then. Hey, why don't you join us? I'm paying. If you can round up more of the old high school crowd, even better. Is everyone over twenty-one? Right, the twins would have been the youngest in the class. We'll start planning the party without the twins. Great!" We set up a time and said our goodbyes.

I felt victorious. It doesn't take much these days. Dianne wore an expression of mild approval, so I felt justified.

"Do you have a salsa dress?" I asked, not bothering to keep the triumph out of my voice.

She closed her laptop and rose to her feet, a glorious sight when she unfolded her almost six feet of grace. "Why would I not?"

# CHAPTER 20

# JD: THURSDAY NIGHT, DICKINSON

Ojos Locos had nothing special to distinguish it from any other tiny salsa club with more sound, people, and booze than dancing space, but that was fine. Elisa had gathered five other female twin-friends, and we all scrunched around one of the tiny round tables. I fetched drinks and smiled like the gringo I am. I brought up the birthday party, and they all talked about what they did for their twenty-first birthday celebrations.

"Does your dad still live in the same house? Merry and Cherry used to have parties there, in that room over the garage," asked Elisa.

I couldn't imagine Dad wanting to host such an event, so I side-stepped with the information that he was getting ready to move and wouldn't want us to trash the place.

At some point Dianne started speaking Spanish in confidential tones, and I pretended I couldn't, the better to eavesdrop. It's amazing what people say when they think you don't understand.

I danced with every woman in our group. It was fun to see expressions of polite endurance turn into delight when they discovered I could dance, thanks to my mother sending me to ballroom dance class on Saturday mornings, when I'd rather have been doing anything else, and a decade's acquaintance with Dianne, who grew up in ballet, folklórico, and Latin ballroom classes. I can't roll a Spanish double-R, but I can roll my hips in Cuban motion with the best of the island boys.

When possible, I questioned them as Merry's clueless older brother and promised them invitations to the party, when and wherever it was.

I worked through the whole crew before allowing myself the luxury of dancing with Dianne. I asked her if she'd uncovered anything useful. I held my hand up for her to twirl, and she obliged with a double spin.

Her eyebrows drew together. "I'm not sure. I've always had the impression that Cherry and Merry were joined at the hip." She tapped hers to mine, which took my breath away. "But according to her friends here, the twins squabbled so much that everyone was surprised they went to the same college."

"Really? It was always them against the world, but that doesn't mean that they didn't argue between themselves. They agonized for two years of high school, trying to pick a place strong in both of their fields."

"According to their friends, both threatened to go to different schools. Often. They've known your sisters for years, since before your mother died—"

My phone chirped, and I checked it, since anything could be important. I sighed. It was Heather, she who talked my ear off the other night. On the other hand, she was part of the case, just as much a twin friend (as far as I knew) as the group here. I held up my phone, pointed to outside, and gave Dianne a last spin as I answered, saying I was moving to a quieter place.

As opposed to dance music, outside was full of traffic noise. I took refuge in Dianne's car.

"I'm sorry to bother you, JD," said a breathless Heather when we at last agreed that we could hear each other. "I've just been thinking about Merry—you sounded so worried the other night. You had to get off the phone so quick, in case she called. I hope she did?"

Was that my excuse to abandon the pointless conversation that seemed likely to go on until the next week? I'd have to go with it. "No, I must have misunderstood her. Didn't hear back from her."

"I tried to call and text her too, but I didn't hear anything back. I asked around too, and no one's heard from her in ages. I wondered if she was okay, and I got to thinking. I might know something. I didn't think anything about it at the time, but if she's really missing—I need to tell you, and you can decide. Are you still in Houston? I'd rather meet up than talk on the phone. It's just not something I want to say—"

"At the moment, I'm at Ojos Locos, somewhere around Dickinson."

"Oh! That's really close to Texas City. Could you come here? This isn't something I'd want anyone to hear. Please. I know it's asking a lot—"

She sounded so sincere and urgent—and I was getting so desperate —that I agreed, saying I'd be there as soon as I could. I pushed my way back onto the dance floor. Dianne disentangled herself from her current partner and whirled herself into my arms. We did some basic, minimal salsa steps in place and up close while I whispered my plans into her ear. Bar smells clogged the room, but this close to Dianne, her smooth skin contrasting with her scratchy spangly dress and her gardenia perfume entwining with her own aroma overwhelmed my sensory world. My words trailed off, as I lost my train of thought.

"Bueno," she said. "Take my car, and I'll get someone to drive me back."

I snapped back into reality. "Oh sure, like I'm leaving you stranded with a bunch of strangers. I'll take a rideshare; it's not that far."

Breaking into side steps, I guided her back to the table, where the heat and the exercise had blotched all the perfectly made-up faces. Grabbing a last piece of quesadilla for the road, I made my goodbyes, full of gratitude and promises.

# CHAPTER 21

# JD: THURSDAY NIGHT, TEXAS CITY

The rideshare dumped me out at one of those rabbit-warren apartment complexes, the ones that call themselves *minimalist*, when *brutalist* or *devoid of everything* might be a better description, with a mission of "How many people can we cram in this space and charge top dollar?"

It reminded me of the sleek monstrosity I moved into as a newly minted attorney. I forked over a good part of my salary under the delusion that I was moving up in the world. I hated the apartment within a week and would have moved back to Casa Cortez on Becker Street, but we'd given up the lease after everyone had finished as much school as they could stand or afford. The lease I signed kept me in my new space, and when I started looking for somewhere else some months later, I grew even more depressed to discover that they were all tiny boxes of poured concrete looking out over other buildings or the construction of the next complex. All furnished with builder's grade appliances, accessories, and trim, they kept their gleaming appeal for six months after they were built. I wondered how much you had to earn to rent space you might want to come home to. With student loans weighing on me, like the rest of my generation, I didn't expect to be able to afford a house until I no longer cared about it.

Heather's place looked older than mine, which meant dreariness had settled deep into the common areas I had to cross to get to her apartment. After buzzing me into the depressing hallway, she welcomed me at her door with the news that she hoped she could move soon, as soon as her store at Tanger Outlet Mall made her a manager, as they'd promised. After all, she had a business degree from community college, unlike the other losers employed at her store.

After noncommittal noises of agreement, I asked, "You remembered something you wanted to tell me about Merry?"

She smiled and gestured toward a sofa that screamed "rental." In contrast to her furnishings, she was dressed to the nines with full-blown makeup, including shiny maroon lipstick. Just the thing for a relaxing evening at home, right? "Oh yes. Please sit down and relax. What would you like to drink? I have a full bar."

"Water," I replied, perching on the edge of the sofa. "Ice water."

She poured me a glass of wine. I resolutely shoved it aside. I don't say it was the literal bottom-of-the-barrel rotgut I drank when I could afford no better, but it sure smelled like it. That made it all too easy to keep my promise to Dianne.

She poured a glass for herself and snuggled up next to me on the couch. My hair stood on end as I considered switching to a chair. Of course, then she'd sit on the arm and end up in my lap. I'd seen this act before.

Many times in my life I'd said, WTF, why not? It would be temporary amusement for all. But I wanted to find my sister, and this young woman claimed to have information about Merry.

But the more I questioned her, the closer she cuddled, until I finally punched a key combination on my phone that I'd never used before, not as the initiator, except when Johnny and I ran tests before we distributed the app to Casa Cortez after Lisa's murder. I didn't know who still had it installed on their phones, but I imagined all my friends from college hearing ABBA sing the opening lines to the chorus of "SOS."

On my end, I heard nothing. I saw just the flash of a message: SENT. Then a brief acknowledgement to everyone as someone answered the call, the only person in range to respond. I relaxed, with rescue imminent, and returned to verbal sparring with Heather.

"So about Merry—" I repeated, dogged in my quest.

"Gosh, when was the last time I saw her?"

"This summer? This year?"

"Maybe early summer? I didn't think much about it at the time, but you sounded so worried that I thought maybe there might be something you should know." She smiled, feral, as she snuggled. "Maybe you can refresh my memory."

I sat up tall, moving even closer to the edge of the sofa. "Where did you see her? Texas City? The mall? Was she looking for a job?" Maybe I'd overlooked a good lead. I should tramp through the outlet stores and see if Merry found a place to land there. Living and working in Texas City would be cheaper than on the coast, but still provide access to her beloved beach, just twenty miles away.

"I don't think—no, that wasn't it."

I was still going to check. "What about the Village, back in Houston?"

"Um, I don't think so."

"Friend's house?"

She grasped at it. "That's it! A party at—gosh, whose house was it?"

We both jumped as a marauding horde pounded on the entry door. Heather mewled in fear, but I thought I knew the horde-imitator. I called, "Hi, honey. Glad you made it."

I jumped to my feet and peered through the peephole in the door. Sure enough, Dianne stood outside, barely controlling herself, her hand on her purse like it contained a gun. It probably did.

I spoke louder. "Heather, it's my fiancée. I asked her to join me when she got off work." I opened the door and jumped out of Dianne's way. "Honey, this is Heather Webster, my sisters' friend from high school. She was going to tell me about her last contact with Merry."

"Hello. I am Lupita Cortez y Jácquez." Dianne stomped over to the sofa and thrust her hand out like a weapon.

I suppressed a smile at Dianne's new personality, a combination of the despised spicy Latina stereotype and a crime-fighting superheroine, plenty of threat under all the bounce.

Heather shrank back before barely touching Dianne's hand. She warbled in a thin voice. "Hello. Would you like—"

"Water." Dianne pulled the nondescript chair forward so she could look into Heather's eyes. "We are so happy you can tell us something about JD's sister. We feel she is perfectly fine, but naturally we would like to confirm that. Please, catch me up. When did you last hear from her?"

Dianne led with the same questions I had, but she spit them out like bullets, firing each one before Heather had a chance to finish her stalling statements. After ten minutes of rapid-fire questions, making me think she could have had a courtroom or police career, Dianne stood up with a snap, making Heather and me both wince at the Amazon looming over both of us. I gave thanks, as I often did, that Dianne was on my side.

"Thank you, Heather. You might have seen Merry at a party at the house of someone you can't remember, maybe in June, but you're not sure, and you haven't had any contact by phone, app, or email. Do let us know if you have any more information."

I hoped her dripping sarcasm wouldn't eat a hole in the floor. As she stalked to the door, I took a second to play good cop, smiling and thanking Heather for a lovely evening. I caught up to Dianne in time to put an arm around my "fiancée's" shoulders before she shut the door with great firmness. I let her lead us to her car in silence.

"Lupita Cortez y Jácquez?" I asked as I hunched down in her car.

"Fiancée?" she retorted as she started the engine.

"Believe me, I needed a fiancée."

"That may be, but Dianne Cortez is not engaged to you."

"I'm happy with Lupita."

"She's dumb enough she just might say yes."

The conversation wasn't going anywhere good. I fell back on "Thanks for the rescue."

# CHAPTER 22
# JD: LATE THURSDAY NIGHT, GALVESTON

Dianne's shoulders shook with laughter. "Glad to return the favor, for me and all the Casa Cortez residents. Were you in physical danger, or couldn't you extricate yourself from an attempted seduction?"

I thought about it. "No physical danger—I don't think, and anyway I'm a lot bigger than she is—and normally I could get myself out of such a situation. But if she had any information about Merry, I wanted it, and I didn't know if I could do that and turn her down—or if not rejecting her would get me the information I wanted. Do you think she knew anything? Really? Did I mess up the best lead I've had so far?"

Dianne snorted. "Absolutely not. I'm willing to bet she hasn't seen Merry since high school. You know, some of the people who came to Ojos Locos tonight work in the outlet stores, some just for the summer, others long term. It's supposed to be a good place to work, for retail. They could have invited Heather, who lives close by. They didn't. I hope you don't mind, but I shared some of the truth with the Ojos Locos crowd. Not all the details we learned from Sonia and finally Cherry, just that Merry hadn't contacted anyone in weeks and we were worried about her."

"I don't mind. I was trying to get an honest answer from the people I talked to—either that, or the sense that they weren't telling the truth.

Not that I have total faith in myself as a lie detector. I didn't want all my witnesses tainted with gossip and imagination. Just ask the police what happens when they set up a tip line."

"I've heard. Maybe .0005 percent of the responses might be valid leads. Everybody else is just making it up. I knew you already had first impressions of this crowd. When I told them you were meeting Heather, they said to take anything she said with a boulder of salt. In high school, she was a chaos agent, spreading rumors, breaking up friendships and relationships."

"I wonder why she was still on Cherry's friend list." When I didn't get an answer, I glanced at Dianne. In the dashboard's dim light, her teeth gently held her lower lip.

"Did you see much of your sisters when they were in high school?" she deflected.

"While I was in law school? Then studying for the bar? I didn't see much of anyone. They always seemed okay when I went home. Just your typical cynical, sarcastic teenage girls. They had no use for a stupid elder brother."

"You never heard about their troubles then?"

"No, unless you mean right after Mother's death. Merry withdrew into invisibility. Cherry went wild and tried to destroy the world. Grandmother got them into therapy for a couple of years. I thought they were fine."

"Yes, if your definition of fine is Freaked Out Insecure Neurotic and Emotional."

"Oh?"

"Or Feeling Insecure, Numb, Empty," Dianne conceded.

"Aren't those definitions of teenagers?"

Dianne tapped her fingers on the steering wheel. "One of the twins hauled off and slugged Heather once."

"Sounds like Cherry."

"Nope. Merry."

I blinked my eyes in surprise. "That needs some explaining."

"Merry was Heather's chosen target for a while. Heather bullied her online and in person, spread rumors about her, especially to Merry's dates. Finally Merry snapped." Dianne pulled her car into the hotel parking lot. The palm trees loomed over us, their topknots threatening dark amorphous shapes high above. "Cherry not only cheered Heather on, but supplied her with tidbits and methods guaranteed to get under Merry's skin. Cherry and Heather thought it was hysterical. Merry got suspended, Heather wore heavy makeup for a week, and Cherry wore absolutely no makeup—Merry put it all through the garbage disposal. Your grandmother said it served Cherry right. She could just save up and buy more—after her allowance was restored, that is. There was some talk about sending the girls to different schools, even having one go stay with relatives for a year, but the next school year, they were both back at Lamar High. I suspect more therapy was involved, but no one there knew what happened—why they fell out or how they made peace."

I frowned with the effort of remembering as we strolled through the lobby. "Sounds like my family, always keeping secrets. Dad told me high school would be the happiest years of my life. Fortunately I knew he was a liar, or I might have felt like killing myself. Did you know any of this before? Were the twins still coming on your hermanas y primas clothes-buying extravaganzas?" Before they could drive, I chauffeured them, but by high school, they were driving themselves.

"Not always, and I remember a couple of times when only one did because the other had an activity, usually one of Cherry's plays. On the one hand, I feel stupid that I didn't notice. On the other hand, my stated goal was to get twenty teenage girls to buy a semester's worth of clothing in six hours that met (1) their budget constraints and (2) their mothers' prudery. I would have noticed someone sitting on the sidewalk crying or girls punching each other out, but not much else, if they just followed the crowd and wore at least half a smile."

"Having been on some of those trips, even as buying wrangler for Zap and your male cousins a few times, I concur."

Dianne sniffed as I opened the suite door. "Oh, boys! So easy, just five pair of the same jeans, one pair of slacks for church. Five shirts, same brand, different colors, for the wild ones."

After the door closed behind us, I dropped a semi-chaste kiss on Dianne's cheek. "For my fiancée, Lupita."

"Lupita's out of the office. Please leave a message." Dianne brushed me away, but not forcefully. "Sometimes Chantal or the other housemates came along to help. Sometimes a few of my tías, because my rule was that I needed another adult for every five girls. Any of them would have mentioned anything unusual."

"So nothing ever? The twins got along?"

"Merry and Cherry shopped at different stores, so they didn't have to interact, not even at meals, when we'd be seated at a table for twenty. JD, what if we're looking at this the wrong way? What if Merry's not Cherry's beloved twin? Cherry was a holy terror at Gregg House, complaining about the work she was assigned, mixing it up with Darryl, who decided she was his assistant. I was relieved when she decided to go back to Waco. I'd been cutting her slack because she had to be worried about her sister. What if she's not?"

Good old Dianne, she who says the quiet part out loud, even though quietly. A growing sense of dread had knotted my insides during the ride back to the hotel, and a monster was ready to claw its way out of my torso. What if everything I thought I knew about the twins, about my family, was wrong? What if Merry had good reasons never to be found? What if—

On two phones, ABBA burst into their hit song "SOS." We both gasped and fumbled our devices in panic.

"Johnny! Johnny?" I exclaimed.

"Somewhere near Waco," Dianne added.

I'm not sure if I offered my arm or I hugged her after she nestled close to me, but we locked ourselves in a desperate embrace while we stared at our screens, as though we could will somebody closer to accept the call.

"What are the odds that both men use the SOS app on the same night?" murmured Dianne.

"Numbers are your department," I replied. "Who's still on the app? Anybody closer to Waco than we are? Someone has to be nearer than our three-and-a-half hours' drive."

Dianne just shook her head.

Our screens stayed dark. I sighed. I knew how this worked. If no one was close enough to accept the call in person, somebody would accept and notify the authorities, if appropriate. Chantal, for instance, said to never call the police if she lay bleeding out on the concrete. Johnny?

Maybe. He wasn't sure whether being one-quarter Vietnamese made him a person of color in the eyes of law enforcement.

The emergency call had come from somewhere in the vacant space between Waco and Austin. The only thing I was halfway sure of was that Johnny wasn't in a difficult social situation. He wouldn't send an emergency call over hundreds of miles for that.

All this ruminating gave me time to see if someone closer would respond. They didn't. I glanced at Dianne, her lips thin and tense. "I'm inclined to notify the police and my grandfather. He's not that far from the site. Any better ideas?"

"Call them both. Then Johnny and Cherry. We don't know if she's with him." Dianne pulled two bottles of water from the refrigerator.

"Let's text, in case the phone ringing would be awkward or dangerous. You contact Cherry; I'll take Johnny." I accepted the water with gratitude. The cold felt good on my throat.

When I was halfway through the bottle, Dianne's phone twittered. She put Cherry on speaker.

"What's wrong?" Cherry demanded. "It's late for you people to be calling."

Dianne's sigh of relief echoed mine. She asked, "Are you with Johnny?"

"He dropped me off hours ago at my place. He was going to make a tour of the jock bars to see if he could find Merry's attackers. Where is he? What's wrong? I just got a text from him saying not to go out on my own, to always have someone with me, and go stay with my grandparents. What's going on?" My sister's voice pitch rose with her anxiety level.

I said, "We don't know the answer to any of those questions. If you gave him a list of places, send them to me too."

"Always with the lists, you detectives."

"That's us, the Hardy Boys and Nancy Drew." I gestured to Dianne to take me off speaker and stepped away to make my calls.

"Trixie Belden," protested Dianne, never a Nancy Drew fan. "We think Johnny might have had an accident. Sit tight and we'll keep you informed."

The authorities seemed skeptical of my emergency, even after I forwarded Johnny's location. I then called my grandfather, who was more receptive. He promised to contact the sheriff's office directly since the location didn't seem to be within city limits.

Dianne signed off from her call at the same time I did. We stared at each other, helpless and not far off hopeless.

"Should we start driving to Waco?" she asked, forlorn.

I wanted to. But I said, "Tempting, but we should know something within the hour. Best to go when we know what we're going for and where exactly to."

Dianne paced the room, now small as a jail cell. I found a Latine music channel on the TV and held out my arms. She walked into me, and we did a fierce cha-cha to "Oye Como Va." But her responses turned sluggish, and by the time we got to "Corazón Espinado," she sagged against me until my arms trembled. She's never been a sagger, and it felt like dragging an SUV with the brakes locked.

"Let's watch a movie," I suggested, slinging her toward the couch. "Something you want to see? *Star Wars 68* or whatever they're up to now?"

"Lotsa action," she mumbled. "Something to keep me awake."

My semi-random choice had action, but it all took place in the dark by people who mumbled. Leaning heavy on my shoulder, Dianne was asleep before the opening credits were done. She'd had a long day, with work, dancing at Ojos Locos, rescuing me from the clutches of the evil Heather, and now Johnny's problem, whatever it was. I didn't want to disturb her, so I just scowled at the screen and checked my phone every thirty seconds, each time with increasing dread.

What had happened to Johnny? Where were the rescuers?

# CHAPTER 23
# JOHNNY: THURSDAY, BEAUCHAMP AND WACO

On Thursday morning Johnny opened his eyes in the hazy transition between night and day and silently said the first words of the Jewish morning prayer. *Modeh Ani:* I am grateful to be alive.

He took a few deep breaths to decide whether that were true today.

On the whole, yes, he decided. But true or not, he would rise anyway and run downstairs to check the three cats in his tiny hospital; they all seemed well this morning. He scooped their food and then recorded notes on their progress for their records. Darryl would later call the families with updates based on those notes. Johnny stroked the head of the stray cat with a broken pelvis and promised her a wonderful life going forward. Before he left for Waco, he'd give her an acupuncture treatment for the pain.

Normally he would hear Dianne stirring upstairs, waiting for him to do their warmups before their morning walk or run. The house cats would be waiting to be fed, not as patiently as Dianne. Today only the cats were waiting, Dianne having driven to Galveston yesterday to find JD. He thought she was overreacting, but he had long ago learned not to compare his feelings to other people's. Dianne would feel better if she could find JD. Therefore, it was best that she look for him. She'd sent a text last night saying that she'd found him and was going to stay in Galveston until he was ready to leave.

Her absence didn't mean he shouldn't keep the routine he shared with her. He did Tai Chi by himself; she would have picked yoga or something from her dance classes for their warmup.

The Gregg House Very Good Kitties (plus Godzilla) sang their breakfast song as he headed out the door. He promised them food when he got back. He wouldn't have minded feeding them early, but his housemates didn't want the house cats to think that breakfast at the crack of dawn was the natural order of life.

He ran through the town, making a big circle around and through downtown Beauchamp, stopping at Ming's Donuts to pick up breakfast for the few people left at Gregg House. He used the time to consider what he wanted to ask Merry's friends. He found it hard to believe that no one had any idea where she'd gone or at least what she intended to do. Maybe they didn't know they knew. That was his job, to tease it out of them.

When he returned to the house, Cherry gave him a resentful look, only partially conciliated by donuts. He'd stressed that he wanted to get on the road early, and she'd complied, which surprised him.

Soon they were on the road to Waco in his ancient truck, suitable for hauling an animal trailer containing bobcats or other wildlife, as his position as assistant animal control officer required, but not a high-status truck. If he'd wondered or cared, Cherry's glance around the tattered cab and torn bench seat would have confirmed that.

She climbed in, inserted her ear buds, and closed her eyes. She treated him like part of her brother's furniture, not someone to interact with. That was fine with him, though he made a mental note to try to engage her when they reached Salado, halfway between Beauchamp and Waco.

Cherry perked up when they passed the first sign to Salado. "We should stop there for a few minutes."

"I didn't allow time for it in the schedule," Johnny replied.

She sighed. Johnny, automatically timing its length, judged it to be slightly more than performative. Did she really want to go shopping? Or did she just not want to get to Waco? The length of the sigh was a good gauge to the level of emotional investment, but not so much the actual emotion involved.

He asked, "Do you need to do some shopping?"

"Well, no, but you can always find something in Salado, Granny says. Whatever it is, I usually can't afford it, but she taught us to always stop there."

"I didn't know. I would have allowed time otherwise. But we set up the meeting with Merry's friends for 10:45. We don't want to be late. In fact, I'd like to be early so that I can watch each person arrive."

"You really think there's a mystery here?"

"I know there's a mystery. We don't know where your sister is. It seems something went wrong with her plan. I don't think she intended to cut off communication with you."

Cherry squirmed in her seat. Johnny interpreted that as a signal that she didn't want to hear his words. But he didn't know what to say instead. The goal of this trip was to talk about Merry and her disappearance, difficult if Cherry wanted to avoid the topic. He didn't want her emotions to take the focus off the friends. Emotions, he had learned, were powerful.

"I'd like for you to be there to interpret what they say and how they act, but not if you find it difficult. In that case, you could step away to take a phone call but stay close enough to hear and observe them."

Cherry sipped her water from her fuchsia-and-petal-pink bottle and winced. "How do I know when to leave?"

"When the conversation becomes about you and your suffering, not Merry's location or plans."

"I don't really know most of these people anyway. They came over to the house sometimes, but they always talked about shrimp and stuff in the water. Merry and I don't have many friends in common. We did in high school, and it didn't work well. I'd like somebody better than she did or vice versa and when they didn't like each other—" She paused for an eye roll. "And don't get me started on dating. Do you know how many guys want to date twins? Do you know how many twins don't want to date one guy together?"

"I never considered that aspect. Have you told anyone that Merry's missing? JD's been telling people that he's planning your joint birthday party."

"Is that just a lawyer thing, that he doesn't want to tell them what's going on? I mean, I told people that my grandmother's sick, and we need to get in touch with Merry right away, on the theory that they probably talked to her recently. I asked them to meet with us so that we could pool everyone's knowledge."

"I believe his justification is that he wants to hear everyone's answer without the panic that would accompany a missing person announcement. Your invention provides more of a sense of urgency without reducing people to panic. I hope."

"How much longer are we not going to panic?"

Johnny didn't have an answer.

They reached Mazzio's Pizza just as it opened. Cherry said it was the easiest place for people to find something they could eat. Johnny admired the salad bar, a throwback to the days of his childhood when salad bars seemed to compete for the most ingredients. Cherry told him that the cooks would make vegetarian pizzas for the buffet on request. So he asked for Fresh Veggie Supreme, Alfredo sauce and spinach, artichoke and pineapple, and olives, peppers, and mushrooms. He had more ideas, but their upper limit seemed to be four. While being polite about it, they promised to put more out later if people claimed the first ones quickly.

Happily for Johnny's plans, the six young women arrived separately between 10:45 and 11:05. Cherry gave a sotto voce description of each one as they approached the table. "Merry's main study partner ... Girl from the English class we took together ... From one of her clubs, I don't know, Future Fish Lovers of America or something ... Our next-door neighbors on the other side of the duplex."

Their appearances ranged from camera-ready-in-full-make-up to just-rolled-out-of-bed-and-don't-care.

Cherry delivered the speech she'd practiced in the car. "Thanks for joining us. This is my brother's friend Johnny Ly. I was visiting them in Beauchamp, and he drove me back to Waco. We're having trouble getting in touch with Merry, and I thought you guys might know something or maybe know something together, if we combine everything."

"You don't think anything happened to her, do you?" asked one of the camera-ready girls.

Cherry glanced at Johnny. She hesitated, as though this part of the script gave her more trouble. "I don't think so, but it's not like Merry to go off and not let people know where she is. I bet she just forgot, or I didn't get her message, but we need to get a hold of her right away because of my grandmother."

The sick grandmother elicited mild murmurs of sympathy. Unfortunately, no one had talked to Merry since the last semester—that also brought out sympathies, since they all knew about her trauma. Merry had told them she was going to take the summer off from school since she had so few courses left in her degree program. They figured she'd do therapy, either formally or with a vacation, and no one had reason to think she would not be back for the start of the semester. Serious about her studies, Merry was already applying to graduate schools.

The conversation was so bland that Cherry never had to step away. Johnny let the crowd wander into their own concerns. After the last goodbye, Cherry grabbed three more pieces of pizza before settling down to compare impressions with Johnny. He noted but didn't comment on her stress eating. The others had taken no more than two pieces, all the while talking about how much they'd have to do to work it off later. They seemed to appreciate the salad bar too.

Johnny felt that even negative information was useful. "Since we have extra time, I would like to try to track down the perpetrators."

Cherry tapped her fork on her plate. "You are kidding, right? There is no way I'm going within ten miles of them."

"I just feel it would be useful to see them. I'm not sure why. JD would call it intuition." He grimaced in distaste. "Can you tell me where their group hangs out? And it would be helpful if you can pull up their photos. I'll go to those places and see if any of them show up. Even if they don't, I might absorb some of their culture and get some leads."

"Believe me, jocks have no culture. Take me home first."

At the duplex she shared with Merry, she gave him a list of likely places and a poster that made his eyes open wider. The heading over photographs of three guys read THESE ARE RAPISTS.

"Did you post these?" he asked.

"Yes, in the women's restrooms around campus. It's been a few months since I put any up. Merry didn't want me to. Do you need anything else?"

"No, thank you." Johnny privately agreed with Merry.

After he memorized the perpetrators' features, he visited each location in turn. The sports restaurants, with multiple TVs set to different stations, made his eye twitch. He wondered if he should take another anti-anxiety pill, or at least his daily can of beer. He decided instead to take a walk between locations, with deep breaths and slow, mindful steps.

Silar University campus was smaller than any he'd attended—University of Texas, Texas A&M, Louisiana State University—but it still had enough people in close quarters to make him nervous. From the time he had arrived at University of Texas, he'd lived first with JD in the dorms and later in Casa Cortez with Dianne, Chantal, and their friends (though by himself in the garage apartment, which made it bearable). Since his Great Unraveling, as he thought of it, during his zoo vet residency at LSU, his previous college years seemed so remote, like they happened to someone else.

He found it difficult to relate to the young people around him as they scurried here and there, even though the semester hadn't started yet. Perhaps that was a good sign. He felt a twinge of compassion for a younger Johnny who drove himself to meet others' demands and schedules, right into burnout. He'd worked hard at shutting out those voices.

The next stop was a place to play games, mostly pool. The sharp crack of an initial break made him wince. He hoped no one saw him slip in foam earplugs. He was willing to trade off possibly missing some conversation for not jumping every time the cue ball hit the full formation. As far as he could tell, the earplugs dampened the sound, not eliminated it. The pool balls slapping each other were more likely to drown out conversation from the card players and board gamers than his earplugs were.

The pool hall would have been a great place to nurse his daily beer, but he called on the stoicism of his Vietnamese grandfather to help him endure while he sipped a soda. Other Texans called it a Coke, but the term bothered him, because not every soft drink was a Coke or even made by that company.

He waited an hour before walking outside again. He found it odd that rush hour noise was more soothing than the pool hall. He drove his truck to the next location, a bar, more of a dive. He found it strange that he liked performing at such venues—there was no predicting where Chantal and Mrs. Cortez would book them—but he'd never willingly set foot inside them otherwise.

As he scanned the dreary menu, his targets walked inside, laughing louder, swaggering harder than the people around him. Rage swelled inside him as the three men made space for themselves—not hard. People automatically backed away.

He watched his emotional progress curiously. Usually, he told himself how he should feel rather than having the feelings themselves. His martial arts teachers had taught him never to raise a hand against someone unless today was a good day to die and take the other person with him. His throat tightened as he became convinced that today was indeed that day. How dare they walk around laughing, when their actions had driven his friend's sister into hiding, perhaps at the cost of her life.

He studied each one, trying to understand how they could do what they did to Merry and laugh about it. He'd learned many things in his year in the college dorm before he and JD moved to Casa Cortez, but he still didn't understand much of what JD shrugged off as *bro culture*. Johnny rose and shoved his way to the bar. Running into one of the rapists, the one with a buzz cut, was not an accident.

"Hey!"

Normally he would have apologized. He didn't. He regarded them as though they were a few levels down from grub worms, though grub worms were useful to the environment. He returned to his booth and drank his soda. Their cheeks turned redder as their emotions flamed.

He set his glass on the edge of Cherry's poster and sauntered toward the door. No one followed him to the parking lot. Disappointed, he loitered a few minutes, but finally climbed into his truck, since the cowards would not attack. Disappointed that he wouldn't be using his martial arts, he aimed the truck for Highway I-35 South to take him back home to Beauchamp.

No sooner had the lights of Waco faded away than lights from an SUV loomed behind, close enough to climb in the cab with him. He sped up. The lights stayed with him. The vehicle tapped his bumper, and he swerved to stay on the road. Yes, the rapists were cowards, but they'd chosen a way to go after him that might leave them unscathed but stood a good chance of killing him.

The game continued, they tapping his bumper and he trying to hug the road. When they darted in front of him, he slammed his brakes and pulled onto the shoulder. That move helped him avoid most of the exhaust they blew back.

As he wrestled to keep from leaving the road altogether, the SUV lights glowed faintly through the dark cloud as it braked to fall behind him once more. He yanked the truck back onto the highway and shoved the accelerator to the floor.

He noticed he was sweating when a salty taste seeped into his mouth. Wondering how long he could maintain his position on the highway, he discovered the answer. The SUV sped up and shoved into his truck one last time, harder and on a curve. He spun out of control and off the road into the grass sloping downward. He focused his attention on keeping the truck upright as it bounced toward the river.

Away from city lights, the night shrouded the surroundings he might have recognized in the daytime. His headlights provided the only visual clues, often too late. His luck ran out after the truck bounced high and smacked into something solid that stopped it in its tracks. The driver's seat belt worked better than the passenger's side. It grabbed him hard enough to make bruises.

Listening so hard his ears hurt, he took a few deep breaths before clawing his way out. He could hear the river—thankfully, close by and not swallowing the vehicle. How long would it take his assailants to turn around and find him? He clicked off the truck's lights, those few that survived the collision.

He wiggled his phone out and sent two emergency calls, one to 911, the other to the emergency app he'd helped develop in college. None of the app's subscribers were anywhere near, but anything was better than sitting in the dark waiting for the people who forced him off the road. He pulled out a large flashlight, the kind heavy enough to double as a weapon, from the small space behind the seat.

His body protested even that mild stretch. It protested again when he reached under the passenger side for the pistol Dianne insisted he carry because he spent so much time in rural Texas and so did rattlesnakes and other dangerous wildlife. As he loaded it, he wondered if he could actually fire it at any living being.

He heard no other vehicles. As far as he could tell, he was alone. More accurately, his truck seemed to be the only vehicle in the vicinity.

He tried to back the truck out. Its gears ground plaintively. It had mated with a large block of stone that Texas leaves about and calls decorative.

He felt vulnerable in the cab. Getting out would provide him more options. Cradling the unfamiliar gun and flashlight, he crept out into the night, lowered the tailgate on the utility bed, and settled himself beside one of the metal storage boxes.

When another vehicle approached, Johnny stilled himself, though he felt as though ants crawled under his skin and demanded that he brush them off. He didn't move. Footsteps approached the cab. He hunched down further. He stared into the darkness and drew a deep breath. He breathed out the Hebrew words, "*Modeh ani*," in case he didn't get to be grateful to be alive the next day.

# CHAPTER 24

# JD: LATE THURSDAY NIGHT INTO FRIDAY, GALVESTON AND BEAUCHAMP

I don't know what woke me up. I had cramps and cricks all over from Dianne's weight on my shoulder and sleeping sitting up. I couldn't tell how much time had passed, but the movie was now a love story, though still in the dark with people who mumbled. My phone had tumbled out of my hand to the floor, fortunately on the rug.

I shifted Dianne over into to a prone position. She nestled into the couch cushion and curled her legs up to her chest. My back and neck complained as I rescued my phone. Anxiety and fear soured my stomach.

I sighed like a wind tunnel when I saw Johnny's text to everyone on the SOS app. I scrolled—and scrolled and scrolled. Johnny thinks you can write a thesis on a text app.

> I am dictating this message as I return with JD's grandfather to Waco. Thank you for sending aid. I called 911 also.

> So did Mr. Thompson. He went to the sheriff's office and demanded that someone accompany him to the accident site.

I don't know why I call it an accident, when I was deliberately run off the road, by Merry's rapists, I believe. The fore and rear cameras on my truck should show the license plate number.

The vehicle tried to cut in front to blow exhaust back at me. I believe they call it "rolling coal." After I swerved into the other lane to avoid the smoke, they then dropped behind to shove me off the road.

Both cameras were operational when I checked and should have uploaded their data to the cloud. Thank you, Dianne, for insisting that I install a front as well as rear camera.

After my truck came to a stop, somewhere near the river, I couldn't start it again. It's being towed into Waco for repairs.

Because I expected the rapists to come back for me, I got out of the cab and waited in the bed. Dianne, I took the gun you made me buy, though I didn't like to use it.

When the law enforcement officer showed up, I didn't know what to do. If they saw the gun, they'd probably shoot. I did my best to hide it.

But I delayed answering the officer until I mouthed part of the Shema. I'd already said the Modeh Ani prayer, but Jews are supposed to die with the Shema on their lips. I wouldn't want to get it wrong.

By that time another deputy and JD's grandfather had arrived. I answered him when he called my name. Relieved, I explained what had happened, and I sent them the camera footage. The LEOs helped me arrange for the truck to be towed.

> Mr. Thompson insisted that I come home with him for the night. I sent a text to Cherry to advise her to stay with them also, but I do not know yet if she did.

> Back in Alvarez County, Sheriff Dane wants me to meet with the Denton family tomorrow to discuss the DNA results received.

> He would like to do so at Gregg House, which has more room for meeting multiple people. So I plan to return to Beauchamp tomorrow morning, one way or another.

I leaned back and let out a long breath. As a singer and high-school trombone player, my breaths last a long time. "He's fine," I said to Dianne.

She drew her knees up even closer to her chin. I went to her room to grab a blanket and draped it over her. I watched her for maybe a minute.

"Sleep tight," I said. I kissed her hair so lightly it didn't move.

Dianne rapped on my door before 10:00 a.m, which saved me from sleeping through checkout time.

"I just talked to Johnny. He's back home already."

"His truck's fixed?" I mumbled after I connected a couple of brain cells.

"No. Cherry drove him. He wanted to get her out of Waco, felt she might be in danger, so she's back with us. Are you going back home now?"

"Yeah. I could keep getting nowhere here for a long time, but I might as well be just as useless at home. You?"

She yawned. "I'll sleep a few more minutes and then head back at a leisurely pace. So much rushing around this week. I'm done."

It didn't take me long to pack, but I thought of one call I should make before I left the area. I got voicemail.

"Hi, Dad. I'm on my way back home. I haven't made any progress. I don't know if you have. Let me know if so."

His voice crashed through as I was finishing my message. "I told you to go home days ago."

"I didn't. I talked to Merry's friends in Houston and around Galveston. I checked out possible places she might have tried to get a job, but no luck. She's not in the New Hire database anywhere in Texas. What about you? I haven't heard from your people, and they haven't contacted the Beauchamp Police Department. Or Cherry. They must work in mysterious ways."

He sneered, so familiar. "Did it occur to you that they might do this for a living and you don't?"

"Not really. I've worked with the police on such cases, and it seems like there's a certain number of questions you ask a certain group of people. As people have pointed out, she'd be great Missing-Blonde-Girl fodder for TV news, but I haven't seen her there."

When I didn't hear a response, I thought we must have gotten disconnected.

Before I could hang up, he said in a different tone, much softer, "I have another daughter, JD. A daughter who looks just like Merry. What will that kind of publicity circus do to her life?"

"Point," I said, feeling silly. I hadn't thought of that.

His voice got even quieter. "My people, as you call them, said their advice about publicity would be different if she hadn't been missing for so long."

"I see," I said, even softer.

So the professionals were looking for a corpse. I didn't want to talk about that. I shuffled off the line as fast as I could and scooted out the door.

I made good time to Beauchamp, just under three and a half hours. Rejecting Dianne's plan for a leisurely pace, I zoomed through a Whataburger and gobbled my sandwich on the road. I parked in front of Gregg House, because it looked like Johnny was holding a convention, and someone had taken my parking spot behind the house.

I was anxious to get to the meeting—Sheriff Dane despises Johnny on the best of days, which this wouldn't be—but I pulled up short when I walked through the front door. The Gregg House ceilings are high enough that I'm always surprised not to see clouds. Today, I did. Suspended from the ceiling were giant, white puffs, probably stuffing from a crafts store. Above Darryl's desk hung a blue sheet draped like a robe, though if it was meant to be a person, their head was pushing through the ceiling. Striped stockings ending in shoes—like Halloween witch legs evoking the Wizard of Oz—peeked out from the draperies.

"Darryl?" I whispered, because shouting would be wrong. I didn't want to disturb the meeting I could hear in another part of the house.

He beamed. "That's for Assumption Day, August 15, you know."

"'Fraid not."

"That's when the Virgin Mary ascended. She was so pure that God took her straight to heaven. It's a good day to pray to her, because she hasn't seen her kid for a while, so he's likely to do what she wants." Darryl always explained religious holidays, no matter whose religion, in a voice of hushed awe. He waved at the ceiling. "So I made an abstract representation of that day. She always wore blue, at least in her portraits."

The more I squinted at the display, the more I could see what he was aiming for. "Abstract, yes. What about the Wicked Witch of the West stockings?"

"I didn't want anybody taking an upskirt photo of her. That would be disrespectful." He spoke to the two middle-aged Latinas who came in the door behind me. "Good afternoon, ladies."

I moved aside to let them through.

The taller woman responded, "Good morning, Darryl. I need flea treatment for my Tigre kitty. My friend Lina and I want to see your Assumption Day display. Father Emilio told us about it after Mass."

As Darryl loped off to the clinic, I eyed the women. They didn't have pitchforks, so maybe Father Emilio hadn't declared a fatwa against us, if Catholics have such things. Of course, they could be packing guns. With Texas laws, you never know, and they had big purses. But they just murmured together while gazing at the Virgin Mary's heavenly ascent. When they both made respectful signs of the cross and bowed their heads over folded hands, I let out the breath I didn't know I was holding.

Darryl bounced back with several boxes that he showed Tigre's owner. "I didn't know if you wanted a single dose, three months' supply, or six months."

"Just a single dose. I like coming in to see your holiday decorations." She handed him her credit card.

"You'll want to come in September for sure. I haven't worked everything out yet—got to run it by the bosses." He paused for a not-exactly friendly look in my direction. "But I know we're celebrating National Ginger Cat Appreciation Day on the first, when we'll have special treats for gingers like your Tigre. Of course, we'll celebrate the Jewish High Holy Days again, and I've got my eye on Mexican Independence Day and Ancestor Appreciation Day. I'm hoping I can talk JD into helping out with National Pancake Day. He makes the best pancakes."

As she tucked the box into her purse, she said, "Oh, I hope he will! And the Jewish holidays were so educational and fun, with the little hut, the unusual plants, and workshops for the children. Lina, you should bring your girls this year." She turned to me. "Thank you, sir, for all this office does for the community. Hardly anyone celebrates Assumption Day."

"We are all about diversity and respect for all cultures and religions in this office, right, JD?" Darryl reached down into a basket by his desk and brought up two blue paper bags tied with cheerful white curly ribbons. "And because Assumption Day is also about blessing the summer harvest, we'd like you to have some of our produce. We've been blessed with so many tomatoes, squash, and cucumbers that we want to share with our neighbors."

The ladies departed with thankful exclamations and promises to return. The last thing I heard was, "And Dr. Johnny is the best vet, and so reasonably priced. You should bring your Toro here."

This was not the law office I expected to have. I knew it was not the accountant's office of Dianne's dreams. But it was hard to argue in the face of Darryl's marketing triumph, repeated every new holiday. I settled on, "Great job, Darryl. I was getting sick of squash for dinner."

"Yeah, well, I'm handing out Assumption Day treats until the squash is gone, if it means doing it until Halloween."

"Carry on."

By this time, I'd figured out that the vague murmurs were coming from my office. That had to mean people were shouting, because with the doors closed, the thick old walls muffle normal-level voices. I decided I could go in my own office, no matter what the meeting.

I blinked at the tableau before me. I could have sworn I'd walked into an old detective novel, where the genius assembles the suspects and picks out a murderer.

Dwarfed by the vintage furnishings, Johnny sat behind my desk. I wondered if he needed a booster seat. He qualified as the genius, but he didn't look like the triumphant, confident, super-detective. His face relaxed as I entered the room. Beside him, Sheriff Dane looked like a toad squatting in the red throne chair pulled in from the gallery. Buddy and Hannah Denton and an elderly man who had to be Hannah's father sat in my client chairs. Two deputies stood against my bookcase, looking official. My office had the most private meeting space in the house, but it felt over-full with all the boiling emotions.

"Sorry I'm late," I said.

The sheriff snarled, "I don't remember inviting you."

"Being part of the justice of the peace office, I don't wait for invitations." I leaned against the nearest windowsill, since the other guests had claimed the chairs.

One corner of Johnny's mouth relaxed. "I'm glad you're here, JD. The Dentons and Mr. Pehr have just learned that the remains found on the ranch are those of Sara Pehr, Mr. Pehr's daughter, Mrs. Denton's sister. We've also heard from Sheriff Dane how she died."

I gave one slight shake of my head. I didn't need to know and the family didn't need to hear it again. Every one of them looked on the edge of explosion or breakdown, as their natures demanded. I could hear the details of her murder later. It had to be murder. She couldn't have buried herself, and an innocent party would have called the authorities.

I felt queasy. Would my family be in this position soon, when a pile of organic material was declared the remains of my sister? Remains. All that remained.

Johnny exchanged glances with the sheriff, who tried to conceal his loathing. Johnny turned back to the family. "Sheriff Dane has asked me to explain the DNA results. Ms. Pehr was identified by her DNA, which matches her sister's." He swallowed. "And Ms. Pehr's daughter Avabella's."

"What else?" demanded Sheriff Dane.

Johnny stared at his hands. "DNA also gives us a clue to the identity of those responsible for her death and burial. The lab recovered DNA from hair on a baseball cap that was left in the grave, as well as a belt, and other items. Though the extraneous DNA was similar, the lab concluded that at least two other people were represented, and those closely related."

"See, I told you," Buddy proclaimed. "That's why you don't want to end up in those databases. The government can make up any story about you."

Johnny plowed through like a John Deere tractor. "One of those people was Avabella Pehr's father; the other, a near relation." He intensified his voice to stage level to be heard through the shouting, the loudest from Buddy. "Commercial databases provided a distant cousin of Avabella's, with a surname of Denton."

Silence reigned as people worked out how Avabella Pehr could have DNA from Hannah's husband's family. Johnny refused to help.

Putting it together, Hannah popped to her feet and screamed, "You fathered my sister's child? You told me you were sterile. You said we could never have children, but you had one with her. You raped her! You probably killed her!"

Buddy shrank in his chair, though Hannah stood at least half a foot shorter than he. "No, Hannah. I didn't. I can't have children. I didn't kill Sara."

Hannah punctuated her screams with sobs. "If you didn't kill her, you buried her. You watched Daddy and me search for her for nine years. You watched us mourn her every birthday and holiday."

Johnny interjected, "I understand Mr. Chuck Denton has been picked up for questioning. He tells the opposite story, that he helped his brother Buddy, who he claims is Avabella's father, bury Sara. He says Buddy killed her after she decided to reveal Avabella's parentage. She was tired of living a lie, a lie she'd have to tell at least for all of Avabella's childhood."

It was Buddy's turn to jump up. "He's lying, that weasel. He killed her and called me to help bury her. I can prove it."

A horrified silence fell over the room, except for the old man's weeping in short, gasping breaths. Sheriff Dane gestured to his deputies, who stepped forward with handcuffs.

Watching the family disintegrate made me light-headed and even more nauseous. Their tragedy extended far beyond the death—murder —of one of them. I clamped my lips tight, imagining similar horrors awaiting my own family.

The front door slammed loud enough for us to hear even with the office door closed. I dove through the door and shut it hard behind me. Whatever new disaster had arrived, it was better than staying.

# CHAPTER 25
# JD: FRIDAY AFTERNOON, BEAUCHAMP

I ran into Avabella, standing by my office door with an innocent expression on her face. While I apologized, Darryl gestured to someone down the hall, and then to Avabella. Cherry trotted down the hall and chirped, "Hey! Let's go look at the cats in the shelter!" Her firm hand on Avabella's shoulder settled the question.

Meanwhile, Dianne fell back against the front door that she'd slammed. She stared upward, aghast. Because the quieter she gets, the more distressed she is, she whispered, "¡Madre de Dios! What is this abomination on the ceiling?"

Darryl chided, "Di-*anne*! Think of the clients!"

I moved as fast as I could towards the downstairs bathroom. No way I was getting involved in that religious debate. Dianne was in charge of questions of Catholicism. Besides, my chicken sandwich threatened an imminent reappearance, thanks to the meeting melting down in my office. What an insult to my favorite fast food. I sank to my knees and waited. Tabby Cat Kee, sunning herself in the window, came down in a spirit of inquiry. She balanced on the claw-foot bathtub and nudged me in a weird rhythm with my clenching insides. Then she made biscuits in my hair. The pinpricks in my scalp drove me to my feet when my stomach stopped heaving. I leaned against the door.

It's amazing how piercing Dianne's whisper can be. "Take that down before tonight's dinner. I don't want half the town to see it."

"Half the town has already seen it, including Father Emilio. He says it makes people think. Told his peeps to make a pilgrimage here. He's coming to dinner too." Darryl couldn't keep a proud note out of his voice.

I headed for the back door. I wasn't up for a religious or artistic discussion. I could imagine me, my family, hearing that a heap of bones was all that was left of our beloved Merry. Would we ever know what happened to her? Would not knowing be better than a clinical description of how her life was ripped away? Or years of wondering and hoping while scolding ourselves out of hope? She might be buried in a shallow grave the next county over from Waco, and, like Sara, be discovered by accident. How could I live with that?

Once in the backyard, I pushed open the door to the octagonal meditation building that Johnny's Jewish grandmother had built for his Buddhist grandfather as a Christmas present. Not that I'm a meditator, but it's quiet, and no one else besides Johnny goes there.

Except for today. Cherry was sitting on the floor with Avabella, who waved a wand toy at the orange cat of her dreams.

"I'm going to name him Sherbet," she said as the cat leaped into the air to bring down the toy, rolling himself up in the cord when he landed. "That, or Captain Citrus."

"What's wrong, JD?" asked my sister.

I must have looked bad, if she noticed. I whispered through clenched teeth, in case the sandwich changed its mind, "They've identified—" I glanced at Avabella.

"Not—" Cherry cried, her face as bleached as those bones in the ground. She lurched to her feet like a zombie, with the same undead expression.

"No, no!" I put my arms around her and looked at Avabella again. I wanted to comfort Cherry without distressing the child. "Another case. Years old."

"Nine," said Avabella as she tossed a jingle ball for Sherbet-Captain Citrus. "My mother's bones. I heard them. Who's my father?"

I shook my head. I partially lied, "I didn't wait to hear." More correct would have been, "I didn't wait to hear which of your uncles it is."

"Somebody in Uncle Buddy's family. I heard that much before Cherry brought me back here to see my cat. I hope it's not Uncle Chuck. He's gross. Do you think Aunt Hannah will let me take my cat home today?"

She seemed calm for a child carrying a ton of bad news. Maybe it wasn't news, just confirmation of suspicions. I answered, "I expect your aunt has a lot to deal with today. But you can come visit him whenever you like."

The cat batted the ball towards the girl and chased it again. When he came within reach, she picked him up and hugged him. "Will we have a funeral for my mother? Gramps always said we would, if she was dead. Aunt Hannah said we'd make big posters of all her pictures with me to put around the church with lots of her favorite flowers, that's tulips, and I'd have a little bracelet of tulips and a dress in her favorite color, that's sky blue, but tulips are never blue. We'd sing her favorite hymns and read her favorite Bible verses, and everyone would know I really did have a mother." Her voice squeaked on the last word.

Releasing her death grip on my neck, Cherry squatted down in front of Avabella and wiped one careful finger under the girl's eye, quite a trick with long fingernails. "Of course you had a mother. And the funeral plans sound—"

As Cherry choked on an appropriate word—no doubt remembering our mother's funeral—I added, on the basis of nothing, "I'm sure your mother would like those plans."

Cherry's voice wobbled. "Maybe you can keep the posters in your room afterwards. That's what my sister and I did after we lost our mother, so we always felt like she was with us." She bowed her head and caught her breath in a suppressed sob.

"How old were you?" asked Avabella, rescuing me from having to respond.

"Eleven." Cherry took a deep breath. "We felt like there was so much we didn't know or remember, especially before she got sick, so we asked our grandmother and our brother to tell us about her all the time, and after a while they felt like our memories too."

"Your dad too?"

"My dad's a jerk. I ignore him as much as I can. The important thing is who you are, who you make yourself into, not your parents or any other relative. They're not always nice people."

I gawked at Cherry in amazement. I'd never seen this side of her. Avabella hugged the cat closer. He trilled a loud meow.

She softened her grip. "The signs in the shelter say you should get two cats, if they're young. Should I get a friend for Sherbet? Will he be lonely while I'm at school?"

Cherry's voice returned to normal. "You'll have to ask Dr. Johnny about that. And your aunt. Would you like to pick out another cat, just in case? We'll take Sherbet so we can see how they like each other."

They returned to the shelter, a remodeled barn next to the meditation building. I watched Cherry's back, trying to reconcile the high school girl Dianne had described to the present compassionate young woman. Which was real? If both, how did they fit together? I took a few deep breaths and decided I could face the world again, in small portions. I walked back toward the house.

I met Hannah Denton coming down the steps. I recognized her clothes, but rage, tears, and now exhaustion had twisted her face into something unfamiliar.

To spare her some effort, I said, "Avabella's with my sister in the cat habitat."

Hannah looked away, as though she'd lost the ability to make any decision.

"Shall I go get her, or would you like her to stay here a little longer?"

"Oh—would it be any trouble? I—have things to do—and I was going to ask her best friend's mother if Avabella could stay with them tonight." She drew a long, ragged breath. "Maybe the weekend."

"You could have your friend pick up Avabella here."

"That would be ... that would be good. But I still have to tell her ..." She reached the end of her capacity.

"She was listening outside the door, and she knows her mother is dead. She doesn't know who her father is or who killed her mother."

An inhuman grimace crossed her features. "Well, I don't either. But I'm going to find out. I'll give them all the DNA they want. Buddy's always been a pig, leaving everything for me to clean up. Now he'll pay for it. I still can't believe—oh, yes I can." In a burst of resentment, she dragged her phone from her purse. "You know, I don't care whether he killed her or buried her. Either way, he's never setting foot in my house again. I wonder how fast I can get a divorce."

Sensing that the moment wasn't right to hand her my card and quote my fees, I went toward the house to give her some privacy. As I climbed the porch steps, she went into the cat habitat, probably to tell Avabella of the weekend's plans and maybe about her mother, easier now that the girl already knew.

## CHAPTER 26

## JD: FRIDAY NIGHT TO SATURDAY MORNING, BEAUCHAMP AND POINTS SOUTH

Dianne met me at the back door. "Zap wants to know if we're going to search for Merry this weekend, because he'd like to come along."

Without thinking, I said, "I am."

"Okay, I'll tell him to set out from Dallas so we can all leave in the morning."

"All?"

"Darryl has to stay behind for the cats' sake, and Chantal's singing in Boerne, but definitely Johnny and me and now Zap. You expected something else?"

Not really.

The kitchen was already cranking into gear to prepare the evening meal. I cursed, remembering it was Friday, time for Johnny's Shabbat dinner. Half the town would arrive shortly for food and ritual. Chantal would sing the candle blessing, and we'd pass around wine or grape juice and braided bread.

I wasn't in the mood for company, but company showed up, including the family of Avabella's friend, and they all stayed for dinner. Johnny was pleased that we had to add two leaves to the dinner table, his measure of social success. The more people who ate his food, the happier he'd be. I considered taking my dinner upstairs to eat on a TV tray.

I didn't, but I didn't talk much either. Eventually people left, and those on cleanup duty—not me—returned the kitchen to a pristine state to await the next assault. Cherry, Dianne, Johnny, and I gathered around the dinner table, now smaller without the extra leaves.

"So where are we going?" asked Dianne. "San Antonio?"

Johnny brought out the old map again and laid the South Texas pieces on the table. He shook his head. "Earlier this week I called a detective I know in San Antonio. I asked her to check the obvious places. She came up with nothing, like we have everywhere else."

I leaned over to study the map pieces. "No one's offered any reason that Merry would go to San Antonio, and if she did, we've got no clue where to start. I'm still thinking she wouldn't want to be hours away from her mail drop in Victoria."

"We've checked every direction from Victoria except south," said Johnny.

"Victoria is a short distance from the Gulf Coast. But we wouldn't be looking at the entire coast, from Beaumont to Brownsville. Assuming no more than an hour-and-a-half's drive from Victoria, we can narrow the search area down from Matagorda on the north to Corpus Christi on the south. One hundred thirty miles instead of three thousand."

Cherry slumped down further. "That's still at least twenty-five towns."

No one pointed out that Merry might not have carried out any of her plans, vague as they were. I didn't say that my hope quotient was in the negative numbers. I was doing this last Hail Mary search just to complete the task, so years later I could tell myself I searched everywhere I knew to search.

I pointed at the map. "These green blobs are wildlife parks and refuges. Wouldn't Merry want to be near something like that? There's five or six of them near those one hundred thirty coastal miles."

Cherry perked up. "Oh, yes! She was really interested in marine ecology before—you know, before. Could we go to those places today, just to look around?"

"Tomorrow," I said. "Victoria is more than two hours south from

Beauchamp. We wouldn't reach any of those other places until after dark. Let's get up early in the morning and set out. Zap will be here by then too."

Dianne tapped on her laptop. "It looks like that map shows the parks correctly, even as old as it is. The most efficient way would be to split up and visit the closest towns first. Unless she was aiming at someplace in particular, that's what she would have done, to minimize driving distance to pick up her mail."

Johnny added, "The police search would have captured the chain hotels and hospitals. We can go by the independent ones, the RV camps, apartment complexes in case she settled somewhere, grocery stores, and restaurants."

I tried not to sigh, not in the face of Cherry's pathetic hope. "All righty then. Which cars are we taking, and who's riding with whom?"

To cover the distance faster, we settled on Johnny and me in my car and Zap, Cherry, and Dianne in hers. Dianne said, without explaining, that it would be best to have a family member in each car. Cherry just accepted it, but I felt sick, thinking about identifying bodies and giving permission for things I'd rather not think about.

The next morning, we loaded both cars with large ice chests of bottled water. I downed one before I started the engine. Texas in the summer. Keep drinking. Water, that is.

Central Texas is muggy, but compared with the coast, it's dry as bread fresh out of the toaster. Like in Galveston, we would feel a breeze on the beach, but not while we tooled around little inland towns at slow speeds.

Johnny and I drew the long straw: southeast from Victoria to Port Lavaca, then on to Powderhorn Lake and Port O'Connor. I drank another bottle of water and watched as Dianne pulled her car out on the road. She, Cherry, and Zap would head southwest down the coast to the Aransas area. It would be a while before they hit any place inhabited.

Wouldn't it be wonderful if it were just me and Dianne, off on an adventure again? As I started my own car, I shook my head in hopes of clearing romantic fantasies, which were better than thinking about the day ahead.

I blasted the air conditioner to the max. Sometimes we swung by drive-throughs for more drinks, as a change from our cooler contents. I gagged on the near-solid outside air when I rolled the car window down.

Johnny kept his eyes trained out the window in search of the elusive green van that Merry bought from her friend Sonia. "I'd rather be searching than sitting around looking at each other, waiting for reports from Officer Al or your father's detective firm. And Cherry will feel better for having done something, however pointless."

Me too.

Port Lavaca was actually a town with streets and stores, but we didn't spot an old green van. We swished through Magnolia Beach's RV parks and one run-down hotel in short order. At this point, I would have ditched the waterfront for a bigger highway, but there were camping areas by the beach, and Merry had told Sonia she planned to live in the van. So we chugged down increasingly deserted roads towards Indianola. Johnny wanted to explore the local history like the Sieur de LaSalle Monument, but I told him to read about it on Wikipedia, if we ever found a cell signal again.

As he apologized for the distraction, I reversed course, both in my mind and on the road, and said we could spare the time. If I couldn't drive away with Dianne, maybe looking at lumps of important stone would keep my mind off the grim possibilities of the day.

The statue of mottled rosy stone rose high enough to exchange greetings with the top knots of the surrounding palm trees. It no doubt made René-Robert Cavalier Sieur de la Salle more handsome and buff than he was in life. While Johnny craned his neck studying the monument and reading the text on all sides, including the base markers—seemed as long as a dissertation—I crossed the street and walked by the water.

Had my sister walked by here recently? Months ago? Ever? I studied the strip of sand, water lapping close enough to let me know that nothing would remain here for long. I scooped up a handful of pebbles, and wherever I saw something out of place—a hair tie; a tattered, colorless ribbon; the remains of a go-cup—I placed a pebble beside it.

Johnny appeared out of nowhere. "Are you going to see the Indianola monument?" He nodded down the beach toward a large plaque—another dissertation—mounted on a pole.

"I—no—I was—" What *was* I doing?

Johnny stared at my work, a pebble by each non-sand item on the beach.

My intent became clear to me. "I didn't have any crime scene flags, so I was putting a pebble by any possible evidence. Like you do at crime scenes."

"Ah. I see." Johnny stooped down to study a lavender hair elastic. "You could take photos and then gather the items, if you want, but the thing about crime scenes is that you know there's been a crime committed in the near vicinity. That distinguishes it from sites of, for instance, tourist litter."

"Just hoping something would mean something," I mumbled, embarrassed. I appreciated having a friend who didn't tell me how pathetic I was being. "We can go, if you've absorbed enough history."

"I like to acknowledge colonial leaders when I have the opportunity." His acknowledgment was a single finger back at the statue.

I nodded in agreement, and we returned to the car.

We were then less than five miles, as the crow flies, from Port O'Connor, the end of this part of Texas except for the long, languorous islands that line the coast. Not being crows, we had to follow the existing roads and backtrack through the Powderhorn preserve.

I gave up on ever returning to civilization. The deep green around us was silent and dense, the air heavy, ripe with odors in this graveyard of marine dwellers. Maybe Merry would call it perfume. I stopped the car from sucking in air from outside. Inside air, after my trip to Galveston and back, stunk only slightly less. I hoped we wouldn't have to search in the preserve. The thick growth gave me the willies, and in August, the rattlesnakes are mean, suffering in the heat like the rest of us. This swamp would have water moccasins too. Maybe alligators, for all I knew. Merry would know.

I wanted to slam my foot on the accelerator, but Johnny kept asking me to slow down.

"It's a great place to hide a dark green van," he said, squinting through the vine-covered palm trees, a change from the Central Texas cedar.

A green van containing a dead body? I ground my teeth. It felt harder and harder to breathe. Either the air grew weightier, or my ribs tightened.

I didn't think it was possible, but they tightened even more when Johnny asked me to stop. He peered out the window for what seemed like a day before shaking his head. "I don't think there's anything van-shaped in there."

I put my foot on the accelerator harder than necessary.

Johnny's head snapped back before he remarked, "But if we find one, I'll investigate it."

I waited for him to tell me he had more experience with death and corpses, but he sidestepped it with, "I am, after all, an assistant justice of the peace."

I knew he wasn't referring to the small claims court or wedding offi-ciant duties, and we both knew he was out of his jurisdiction.

I remembered that long-ago day, back in college, walking with Dianne through an endless field as we searched for Lisa. We both breathed harder as the sun glared down. In the company of strangers, we trudged for hours. I was so bored I longed for it to be over, like now, but terrified of what *being over* meant. When the shout finally went up some fifty feet away, I shut my eyes tight and pulled Dianne to my chest to block her gaze. She swore at me in Spanish and broke away to see what was left of her friend. I ran and caught her as her knees gave out. I wondered who was going to catch me.

And Cherry. Who would catch her? I knew the answer: Dianne.

"Maybe we should go back to the entrance of Powderhorn RV park and try to get information," Johnny mused when we reached the blessed exit from the preserve back onto a state road. "Maybe Merry was there earlier. This seems like the kind of place she would love, with all the water and marshland."

I pulled over, got out to stretch, and retrieved several bottles of water. I had too many warring impulses to answer him right away. My mouth was dry from swallowing hard every time Johnny asked me to slow down. I handed him a bottle and swilled down another. The chill felt good. "I'm not going back through that horror show now. Let's go on to Port O'Connor, and we can stop in the RV park on the way back."

"Do you want me to drive? You don't look well."

I thought about it as I reached for another bottle. "I'd rather drive than do the searching and coordinating. You can drive us home."

We found cell service when we reached what I was happy to call a highway. An hour ago I would have called it a cow path. Several messages from Dianne poured through, reporting nothing, just as successful as we were. I tried to decide whether that was good news.

# CHAPTER 27
# JD: SATURDAY, PORT O'CONNOR

The welcome sign to Port O'Connor said Visit to Fish. Return for Life. I took that as a threat. The only road in felt like the back way, with scattered houses and businesses gradually increasing to almost a town. Water surrounded the place on three sides: Boggy Bayou to the north, Barroom Bay to the southeast, and Espiritu Santo Bay to the south, with the Gulf of Mexico grumbling just beyond the skinny islands sheltering the coast. The buildings perched on stilts made me nervous, reminding me that hurricane season loomed large. I wouldn't want to try to evacuate on the single two-lane road leading out of town.

Still, I entered Port O'Connor relieved, almost cheerful. This journey was almost done. We would fail, go home, and start the long wait, maybe forever. But we *would* quit driving through fish-stinking villages by the bays and on the coast.

Port O'Connor wasn't even a quarter the size of Beauchamp, barely thirteen hundred people. In my college days, I'd have thought it a great place for spring break, a place to get sandy and oily and fried to the gills.

At least ten RV parks and an equal number of hotels lay scattered among the bait stores and water sports shops. I tried not to groan. On the upside, they were all within a block or two of each other with parking lots small enough to spot a green van at a glance.

While every plant in Central Texas had died of heat stroke, this coastal area had massive oleander bushes, bristling with poisonous fuchsia, pink, or white bouquets. A smaller shrub loaded with delicate yellow trumpet flowers proliferated everywhere.

"What are those yellow things?" I asked. "I've seen them in Beauchamp and Austin too, but I can't remember their name."

"Esperanza," said Johnny. "It means hope, you know."

I snarled words I wouldn't want my grandmother to hear. Hope and I were done for good.

As I drove down the beach, our prospects grew further apart. We found one motel a block from the beach that was built in the famous Texas box architecture style. The long rectangle squatted flat on the ground, not advisable on coastal land. The back side of the long strip showed ten or so doors, all glowing a fresh, bright tomato-red, matching the cheap window trim. The front side had a lobby, a larger room with a big window and a glass door facing the street, and only six rental rooms.

All expense had been spared to cover the cinder blocks in a rough, pebbly finish and paint them bright white. Heavy rain would wash right through the building, and probably had. I gritted my teeth and turned into the entrance to drive around, as I'd been doing for every place that met our criteria. Let this be the last one, I sort of prayed.

I turned to travel down the back side, down the unbroken row of flaming doors. I slammed on the brakes when I saw a green van parked on the far end, with no exit to the street.

Johnny said, "The license plate matches what we received from Sonia."

We stared for a few seconds. Waves grumbled in the distance.

Sweat tickled my upper lip. "I'm going in the front, and I'm going to ask to leave a message for Merry Thompson, and, and … just see where it goes from there."

Johnny nodded as he popped the door open. "I'll get out here and examine the van."

I returned the car to the check-in area. The red-orange trim glowed in the fierce sunset. Gulls cawed, whether warning or encouragement, I couldn't tell. Now the smell of fish was so strong that I could taste and feel the oily texture in my throat.

I had one line to say, but I kept rehearsing it. I pushed the front door open, into a room with a couch and a few chairs that weren't antique or vintage, just old. Behind them was the long check-in desk of battered wood. The young woman behind the counter looked up as I said, "I'd like to leave a message ..."

I stared. She stared back.

The hair was brown. The eyes were brown. Her blouse hung loose and flapping, unlike anything I'd ever seen her wear. But she was my sister—flabbergasted and anxious, but my sister.

I'd been holding my breath, and I could only squeak, "Merry?"

I held out my hands, not sure she wanted anything to do with me. She ran from behind her desk and flung herself into my arms. I squeezed her tight as we babbled at each other, neither making any sense. I broke the hold to step back and look at her. She gestured to the dull-brown couch. We sat down together, arms and hands tangled.

When Johnny walked through the front door, I thought his grin would wrap around his head. He tapped his phone in a fury, summoning the other troops, no doubt.

Gesturing to her loose clothes, our hands still entwined, I asked, "Why did you leave? Please don't tell me it was because you're pregnant —if you are. It's not the 1950s."

Merry looked down at her stomach. "I didn't know I was pregnant when I left. I was starting to suspect, but I hoped I was just late from the stress and then gained weight because of all the stress. I left because Cherry was going wild, trying to bring me justice, she said. I never knew what she'd do next. I thought she'd stop if I wasn't there. And I just wanted to get away, not deal with my life anymore."

"I heard about the final exam she took for you. And the posters."

Her face turned the same shade as the doors and window trim. "Those posters! She put the guys' photos under the words THESE ARE RAPISTS, and she and her posse put them up all over school. I heard them say there was at least one in every bathroom on campus. I was afraid she or her friends would get in trouble, or hurt. I was afraid of everything."

"Are you going back to school in the fall?"

She hunched her shoulders and bowed her head. "After ... afterwards ... the school wouldn't do anything. Those guys are still there. My rape kit didn't get tested—there's such a big backlog—so it was just their word against mine, the school said. I have only one semester left, but I just can't ... Here I can get up every morning and do this job, even when I'm sad or tired, but when I think about going back ..." She trembled.

"How did you get this job?" I asked to deflect her thoughts.

"I drove from Victoria until I reached the coast, and I stayed here for a week or so, just walking on the beach. They had a sign up to hire an afternoon front desk person, and I told Shyam, the manager, I'd like to apply, but I was running away from abuse. He contracts with this guy Alonzo for housekeeping and janitorial help, mostly undocumented workers. Shyam just pays Alonzo, and Alonzo pays the workers—not very much, but what can they do? And he said he'd take me on as a contractor too, so nobody could trace me. How did you find me?"

"Mostly dumb luck. I spent last week traipsing around Houston and Galveston. We—and Dianne, Cherry, and Zap Cortez—have been driving up and down the coast this afternoon, hoping we'd see the van." I told her about our detective work, but she wasn't listening.

She gasped. "Zap? Zap's here? Why?"

"He wanted you to go with him to his cousin's wedding. Cherry said you had to work and went in your place. He was worried when nobody knew if you were okay."

Merry looked down. "I went out with him a couple of times before ... I hoped—but I can't think about that now."

"Of course not," I said.

Johnny's voice startled both Merry and me. He'd been so quiet, leaning against the wall on the far side of the room, that we'd forgotten about him. "And JD figured out that you'd want to be near marine wildlife preserves or parks. There's quite a few within driving distance of Victoria."

Merry opened her eyes wide. "Wow! That's really clever, JD. I always visit one on my day off. I've just started repeating some of the bigger ones."

I squeezed her hands. "If you're driving all over the place, why didn't you pick up your mail in Victoria? The post office box was full.

That finally convinced Cherry that something happened. The rest of us freaked out as soon as we learned Cherry had been impersonating you since May. Why didn't you answer your phone, the burner?"

Merry made a face. "The cheap thing broke. It's still in warranty, and I thought I could get it replaced in a few days—I didn't think Cherry would notice I was offline—but it's been more than a week now."

"Always the way it is with warranty replacements," I sympathized.

"I had asked one of the housekeepers if I could use her name to get a replacement from the company. She has the same model phone, and I'm going to give her some of the minute cards Cherry sent me."

"Won't you need to go to Victoria to get them?"

"Yes, but I don't have any privacy here. I'll go to Victoria when I need more money or minutes. Shyam lets me live here in the room he uses for storage. People have obviously slept there before, maybe the housekeeping staff hiding from Immigration and Customs. After I found the room searched, I started keeping most of my stuff locked in the van and carrying the cards and my ID with me."

I dropped my voice low. "Merry, your family loves you. Couldn't you tell me, at least, if you didn't want to tell Dad? No one could blame you for that. But with all Dad's faults, he has money and health insurance, which he'd be glad to share with you. Were you that scared of those guys?"

She wiggled, just like the tween I remembered. "Not exactly—maybe—I didn't want to leave a trail. I didn't want you to know. I thought you all would tell me to get an abortion. I took the Plan B pill, but it didn't work. Maybe it was too late. After that, I just couldn't decide. It's like I'm two people: one searches for abortion clinics and saves money for it. The other eats right for the baby, doesn't drink, takes vitamins, and goes to the clinic every month and follows their advice. Every time I try to plan, either way, I cry. I just don't know!"

"Of course you don't. PTSD isn't just for soldiers. One of the symptoms is not being able to make decisions. I'm not going to make that decision for you—I can't answer for Dad—but I want it to be what you want, not what seems best or smartest, but what you really want. Maybe you can figure that out with counseling. You need prenatal care too. Dad can get both for you."

"I have both. I go to a clinic for poor people every month. And a counselor, too, from a church I passed on one of my walks."

"Not one of those churches that thinks every sperm and egg, particularly joined together, are sacred?"

For the first time, she smiled. "No. A Methodist church, just like we grew up with. It's so good to have someone to talk to."

I was both glad and wistful that she turned to faith for solace. "You're doing great. But you need to let Dad know how you're doing. He'll want to see you."

"No! I'm not going home, and I don't want him here. This is my place! I don't want to talk to him either."

"Do you want me to talk to him? If he insists on seeing you, we could make it neutral territory, at our place in Beauchamp."

Shaking, Merry nodded. She crumpled against me as I took out my phone. Wrapping my arm around her, I flashed back to the days when everybody's favorite thing was to send me to an evening movie with my sisters: they were thrilled to stay up past their bedtime, our parents were thrilled to have an evening to themselves, and, even though I'd rather have seen something besides Disney Princess XXXII, there was at least a chance Merry and Cherry would fall asleep, one on each shoulder, leaving me free to play games on my phone.

"Hello, Dad? We've found Merry. She's okay." I waited for the shouting to die down before giving him a flat, dry Cliff Notes version of Merry's last months, like I was summarizing for a judge. Merry flinched at every sentence. Johnny, who'd been doing a most excellent imitation of the wallpaper—his specialty—went out to the car and fetched water for all of us.

Like I figured, Dad insisted on seeing her, right now. I put him off to the next day, back in Beauchamp, if Merry could get off work. That led to more shouting, so I hung up and texted:

11:00 a.m. Unless you hear otherwise

We sipped our water in silence until we heard voices from the parking lot. The commotion brought both of us to our feet, Merry going back to her desk, me heading for the door in a moment's confusion that it had to be Dad arriving. I soon saw the rest of our team, all trying to get through the door at once. It looked like Dianne was going to win, because, you know, Dianne, but Cherry ducked and wiggled through to sprint into her twin's arms. Plastered together, they wept in chorus. Dianne put her arms around both, and her brother stood to one side, as though he'd like to join but didn't dare.

Zap came to stand with Johnny and me, while the women flowed onto the couch, hugging Merry in the middle, all crying as Merry told her story again. It wasn't the first time I was jealous of feminine tears, but I didn't feel I could join the crowd on the couch. For one thing, there was no room.

Johnny stepped to the front desk to retrieve a handful of tissues, which he gave to the men. "It certainly is a sweaty day."

He dabbed his forehead, and Zap blotted his neck. Funny how all my sweat was under my eyes.

# CHAPTER 28

# JD: SATURDAY, PORT O'CONNOR AND BEAUCHAMP

Merry retreated behind her check-in counter and tapped a button on the motel phone set. Apparently she summoned the manager because he arrived within a minute. His eyes widened when he saw Merry's entourage. Still, he gave Merry three days off when she told him about a grave emergency in her family.

Cherry volunteered to sit at the front desk while Merry packed—she didn't want to leave anything behind in her room. While she did, I called our grandparents to catch them up. I tried to be tactful and Grandfather tried to gloss things over for Grandmother's sake, but she brushed him aside and demanded every detail I could provide. I invited them to the family meeting the next day in Beauchamp. I hoped they'd keep their son in line. That guy is just too much.

Merry didn't want to leave her van behind either, so Johnny took off in my car. We Thompsons piled into her van with me at the wheel and the two sisters in back, leaving Zap and Dianne to return in her car. Before we set off, Merry opened the window to lean out and beg Zap to come to Beauchamp too. He promised he would and then pulled out all the Old World courtesy of his ancestors as he reached for her hand and kissed it. Cherry covered a giggle and pulled her speechless, blushing sister back into the van.

On the way out of town, Merry acted as tour guide, pointing out sights of interest. "Isn't this just the kind of place Mommy used to take us?"

It was.

They huddled in the back, twinning all the way, whispering in the abbreviations, expressions, and hand signals known in the family as twin-speak. Cherry provided sobbing background vocals.

"I tried so hard not to let you down, to keep your secrets. I wanted to prove I was better than I was in high school, when I believed all that garbage Heather put out about you."

"Heather!" replied Merry, stuffing the name like a Thanksgiving turkey with scorn. "Thank God Granny took us to that counselor the next summer."

"I promised I'd always believe you over other people, that I'd defend you and support you, and I tried, but then I saw all those envelopes at the mailbox and I thought, I thought—JD had this other case about some bones in the ground that he was trying to identify for a family. What if that was you?"

"I didn't think anybody would notice when the phone broke," Merry cried. "It was only supposed to be for a few days."

As they swirled downward in floods of tears, I offered a distraction. "I ran into Heather this week."

It worked, changing their sobs to vitriol.

Cherry declared, "I don't say you have to marry Dianne, JD—"

"But you'd be an idiot not to," chimed her sister.

"—but if you ever even go out with Heather, you are dead to me."

Skirting the first part of her sentence, I made the easiest promise of my life and vowed never to have anything to do with Heather. "Cherry, why did you include her in the high school friends list you sent me?"

Merry squealed, "You didn't, Cherry! JD, did you talk to every one of our friends? How embarrassing! I can never go back to Houston again."

Cherry responded, defensive, "I never ghosted her because who knows what she would have done behind our backs. But I forgot she was there. Don't worry. JD told people he was planning our birthday party."

"Yeah, we need to do that. Heather's not coming, though."

After wrestling that subject, Merry and Cherry moved on to trading summer stories: the untalented idiots Cherry dealt with at her internship, the time Merry hid undocumented housekeepers in her room while ICE officers pounded on her door.

"They were shouting at me to open up. I yelled back that I didn't have to, I was an American citizen, and everybody in my family was a lawyer, and I was calling my brother and my dad right now. They could have kicked the door in—anybody could—but they went away. Jaya and Cristabel stayed in my room for the next three days. For a week, I called the front desk before I went out, making sure the coast was clear. I did housekeeping for a week because people were afraid to come to work."

My little sister was growing up to be quite a warrior. I'd make sure she took back some of my cards, since I had a grant to defend immigrants in court.

The next morning at Gregg House, I made pancakes for everybody, with eggs from the neighbor's chickens and blackberries from our yard. Johnny tended his patients while the rest of us toured the buildings, gardens, and cat shelter, which made for light work, because everybody wanted to take care of the cats. Darryl, having cared for the cats all by himself until that day, was particularly glad. Merry helped in the garden some, but she found bending uncomfortable. Cherry looked at her sculpted nails and sniffed a refusal, though she picked a few blackberries.

"Remember how we did this with Mommy?" Merry exclaimed, pulling vines aside, avoiding the slender piercing thorns, to find the fattest berries.

We did.

We were playing with the Very Good Kitties in the living room-hallway when the doorbell rang. Merry and Cherry froze on the yellow-gold sofa, Zap and Dianne leapt to their feet to make an exit, and Johnny, still in his white vet's coat, leaned against the far wall, preparing to be invisible.

On the way to the door, I grabbed the squirt bottle and sprayed Ginger Tom, who'd snuck away from his siblings to attack the orchid Dianne kept trying to grow on the reception desk. When I opened the door, Grandmother pushed past me. In seconds, she was on the sofa with Merry in her arms.

I stepped in front of Dad and Grandfather. "This is just to say that anyone who raises his voice or says anything negative whatsoever to Merry, including but not limited to 'What were you wearing?' or 'How could you let this happen?' is getting squirted like a common kitten. Down, Ginger!" The cat spoiled my menacing tone by sneaking back onto the desk for another go at the orchid.

Dad's ice blue eyes met mine.

I smiled, anticipating the pleasure.

Grandfather huffed as he pushed past. "Nobody's going to be unkind to her." He strategically claimed the red chair, farthest away from the sofa.

Dad stood in front of the twins. Cherry hunched over, her knees pressed together like she was ten, but Merry sat upright and met his gaze. After all, the worst had already happened to her. Hoping it was true that you could turn a tragedy into a comedy by sitting down, I shoved one of the yellow chairs behind my father.

He'd pickled his emotions long ago, but he must have been feeling a few, for he couldn't speak for some time. I pulled up another yellow chair beside him for myself, where he could see the spray bottle.

He gave me some side-eye before opening his mouth to speak, but Grandmother beat him to it.

She announced, "She's coming home with us."

"Today?" asked Grandfather, surprised.

Merry shook her head. "No, I'll go back to my job and give notice and come back in a few weeks, if I still think that's the best thing to do. I guess that's how I make decisions, just keep on going until I know for sure."

"Solvitur ambulando," said Johnny. "That's Latin for 'It is solved by walking.' Time-honored tradition."

"That's it exactly!" exclaimed Merry in relief.

Dad had clearly been turning over approaches. He came up with: "You're having the baby then?"

Merry winced. "I haven't exactly decided, but probably. It's almost too late to do anything about it. I'm not sure about adoption."

He glanced at me and then back to Merry. He asked, in as gentle a voice as I'd ever heard from him, "You feel you can raise your rapist's baby?"

I fingered the squirt bottle. If Merry broke down—

She didn't. "I'm not sure yet. I'm talking to my counselor about it. What happened to me isn't this baby's fault."

"Any decision you make will be yours alone. You'll soon be twenty-one, an adult in every way." I worked on a casual tone.

Dad's face showed his fight not to tell her that he knew best. First time I ever saw him resist. "Of course your family will support your decisions. It's not what I want for you, to be tied down so young, but —" Starting to lose the fight, he glanced at me and then back to her. "What about school?"

Merry looked torn. "I don't know if I can transfer somewhere else without falling way behind, but I shake every time I think about walking on campus again."

I cleared my throat. "Maybe, if you don't have labs, you could take your last classes remotely. I'll ask for you; I have several things I'd like to ask the administration of that school. Maybe some of the other lawyers in the family want to join me."

"Yes," Grandfather agreed, in a voice that would have had those administrators resigning, could they have heard it.

Avoiding her sister's eyes, Merry looked at me. "I don't want to talk to the administration again. Not ever. But if you're going to ask, would you also ask if I can take my finals over? I was pretty upset, and it shows in my grades."

Dad's eyes gleamed as he spotted something he could do. "Of course I will. You, getting a C minus!"

Merry squeezed Cherry's hand as they both looked at the floor. "I felt lucky to get it at the time, but I know I can do better."

In his tombstone-courtroom voice that boded no good for some-body else, Dad said, "I feel sure they'll be all too happy to give you what-ever we ask for. JD said the rape kit wasn't even tested. I can make that happen, if I have to pay for it myself."

Johnny, unseen by most of the room, spoke, making the rest of us jump. "It would be a good idea to test all the backlogged kits, at least the recent ones in the university area. Rape tends to be a serial crime. I expect you'll find several DNA matches."

Cherry looked up. "That's true. When we were putting up posters—"

"Posters?" asked Dad.

"My friends and I put up posters all over campus with these guys' photos, saying they were rapists."

"I told you not to do that," muttered Merry.

"Well, we did. And other girls came up to us and said it was true, it happened to them too, but the school never did anything."

Grandfather spoke, "We could get the family foundation to pay for the testing, if necessary."

"We have a foundation?" I asked. "What does it support?"

Grandfather gave me one of those looks. "Whatever we want."

I nodded. "*That* kind of foundation. Tell you what: set up crowd funding to test the rape kit backlog, with matching funds from the Thompson Foundation. Advertise heavily on campus—maybe Cherry can make more signs. People can donate in honor of a victim."

"Survivor," said Merry, raising her head.

Dad looked at me and then back at Johnny, as though we weren't half as stupid as he'd thought us, which probably wasn't possible anyway. "Thank you, boys." He caught himself on the last word. Reaching his daily quota of decency, he turned his witness glare, the one he used to sear their souls, on Cherry, who'd deceived and robbed him all summer. Any minute, steam would come out of his ears.

I held up the squirt bottle, supposedly at Tabby Cat Kee, daring to put a claw on the sofa. "My words apply to both, Dad. Merry and Cherry are my heroes."

Merry twitched a smile at me, but Cherry broke down in great gulping sobs. Grandmother immediately scooted over to where she could hug the other twin.

"So hard for you, Charity Adrienne, all you did for Merry with not even her to talk to," she murmured into Cherry's cherry-tinged hair.

I looked at my bratty sister with different eyes. Merry wasn't the only twin who'd found her courage.

# CHAPTER 29

# JD: FRIDAY, A FEW WEEKS LATER, BEAUCHAMP

The twins decided to have their birthday party at Gregg House. Well, if you can't be in Paris, I'd say Gregg House in Beauchamp is the next best place to be.

Having been servers at our county-wide holiday open houses, my sisters knew we had fifty cots to set up in the attic and basement (because Gregg House acts as the town shelter during disasters). Their friends could drive in from Waco and the Houston area and stay the night, always a good idea if alcohol is involved, as is usual at a twenty-first birthday party.

They scheduled the party on a Saturday a few weeks after school started. We assembled our families with a private dinner the night before. Because this intimate little celebration for our nearest and mostly dearest numbered twenty-six, plus the townspeople who always show up for Johnny's Friday night dinners, we asked the guests to bring something for the meal. That might not have been a good idea, because the kitchen was full of people shouting as they warred for space, oven time, and utensils to finish preparations. Having a deadline didn't help. We were simultaneously trying to make last-minute preparations for the next day's party and get the celebratory dinner on the table by sunset, the start of the Jewish Shabbat.

Zap had driven an SUV full of sisters, cousins, food, and zinnias from Garland. He wheeled in a cart stacked with buckets of the splashy flowers and presented them to a wide-eyed Merry.

"... and for your sister, of course." Zap blushed, searching for Cherry, who'd already disappeared with Juke, Tima, and the food they'd brought. "My mother sent them. She wanted to come tonight, but she had an event."

Merry matched his blush. "Thank you—her. They're really pretty. JD, what should we do with them?"

"Dig out every vase we have and then wrap any buckets left with wrapping paper." I'd had experience with Mrs. Cortez and the flowers she acquired from wholesale dealers, because why have one flower when you could have one or two hundred? Seeking to escape the escalating Kitchen Wars, I offered to take over floral distribution.

Avabella and Hannah Denton arrived in the midst of the chaos for an appointment with Johnny. I met them as they walked through, each carrying a cat carrier, as I carried vases of sharp-scented zinnias around the gallery.

Avabella announced, stuffing the first two words full of pride and love, "My mother said I could have two cats, so they wouldn't be lonely. She's adopting me, and I'm adopting them. So now I'll have a real mother, and they'll have a real home."

"Congratulations to everyone," I said, meaning it, as I peeked in the carriers, where one orange tabby and a smaller black-and-white tuxedo cat were not sure about the change in their circumstances.

"So many people! Are you having a party?" asked Avabella.

"We are. Tomorrow's my sisters' birthday."

"Cherry? Mommy, can I go tell her 'Happy Birthday?' She was nice to me."

"Cherry!" I called upstairs, where the twins were setting up the rooms for their friends. "Someone to see you!"

Avabella set her carrier down with tenderness and took off as soon as Cherry appeared at the top of the stairs. I blinked away a memory of the twins at that age, exuberant, never walking when they could run, certain that life held only the best things for them, despite already having evidence to the contrary.

"She seems to be doing well," I said to Hannah. "What about you? You lost your sister—but so much more."

She tried to smile and couldn't quite make it. "Honestly, things are better. At least they will be. Now everything makes sense. I told Avabella in her counselor's office, and she said she'd never liked Uncle Buddy and Uncle Chuck was weird. She was glad they were gone for good, and she didn't need a father if that's the best there was." She swallowed. "I decided I'd take the same attitude about husbands. I was running the farm anyway, and now I don't have to tiptoe around him. The money will go further, too." She started to say something but changed her mind. "Did you hear? His brother Chuck was the one who fathered Avabella and killed Sara, choked her with his belt—which he left in the grave—and slammed her head against the wall until she died. Buddy's charged with being an accomplice, and I don't care. He's never coming near us again."

Avabella tore back down the stairs. "Mommy, Cherry invited me to her party tomorrow night. We can come, can't we? She invited us for dinner tonight too, but we should get the cats to their new home. They don't like the carriers."

A duet of feline yowls confirmed that opinion. Hannah looked like she'd like to join in.

I added my voice. "Please do come. Tonight we're having the twins' favorite foods, but tomorrow night we'll serve something from every restaurant and food truck in Beauchamp—barbecue, Asian, Mexican, donuts, pizza, the whole lot. You're sure to find something you like, and Johnny always fixes some special diet dishes. The guests will be mostly college kids, but they'll be tame early in the evening."

"Please, Mommy!" Avabella tugged on the arm that didn't have a cat carrier.

Hannah murmured an acceptance with a wan smile as she directed her new daughter out the front door. The last thing I heard as Avabella danced down the porch steps was, "I'm going to make her a birthday card."

I sent a general hope to the universe that they'd be all right. I felt a wash of survivor's guilt that my sister was restored to me alive, though traumatized, while Hannah had to bury her sister's bones and see her husband and brother-in-law tried for murder.

Dad interrupted my musings a few minutes later, bumping through the front door with the ice cream cakes I'd asked him to pick up from The Sweet Shoppe (one strawberry, one peppermint on a BOGO deal, a present from the store owner). Chantal and Darryl grabbed the foam coolers from him. Before they could run off to put the cakes in the freezer, I detached the birthday cards Alexandra had taped to the tops. Darryl had a birthday card display on the fireplace mantel under a forest of paper streamers hanging from the ceiling. They glowed in bright zinnia colors of yellow, fuchsia, red, and purple. I should appoint him Chief Lightbulb Changer for Life, if it's that easy for him to decorate the twelve-foot ceiling. We drew the line at glitter, though. That stuff sticks around forever.

Dad scowled after them as he followed me into my office. "I don't know why you had me bring ice cream across Texas when the thermometer is bumping a hundred degrees."

"Because the twins wanted something from The Sweet Shoppe, like they had for every birthday when they were little. Because Alexandra, the manager-owner, wanted to give them a present. I'm sure she knows how to package her wares to survive the Texas heat."

Dianne stepped in and shut the door behind her. "I talked to my family, and we're having our winter shopping trip the Saturday before Thanksgiving. We'll give a surprise baby shower for Merry then too, and of course we want both of you there."

My father looked up to heaven, or at least the ceiling.

"Yeah, Dad. You too," I said.

"She wouldn't notice if I were there," he objected.

In her coldest voice that could still be called polite, Dianne remarked, "She would certainly notice if you weren't."

I nodded. "Best to come down on the side of too much support than not enough."

Dad looked out the window at the parched lawn and drooping crepe myrtles. "I thought your mother would be doing this kind of thing."

"Of course she would, but that wouldn't excuse us from our part," I responded.

He gave me a dirty look and left the room.

I looked at Dianne, chewing on her lower lip. "Thanks. For the baby shower, for being a better sister to my sisters than I was a brother, for whipping my father in line without tearing his head off, though I understand the feeling."

She looked directly into my eyes. Few women are tall enough to do that, and none have a laser gaze that can cut diamonds and hearts. "JD, you have to stop looking at me like that."

"Like what?"

"Like you're going to shuck both of us out of our clothes and kiss me all over, starting with—"

I covered my eyes, which wouldn't prevent me from smelling her perfume, those luscious gardenias. "Stop, Dianne. I didn't know I was doing it." I made an attempt to look into her eyes as well, but my gaze wobbled, unlike hers. "I'm sorry. I'm still messed up from this last month, and I feel ..." I floundered for a description. I felt a lot of ways, all contradictory.

Her voice was more tender than her eyes. "We all are. I'll ask my girl-friends if you can come with me to our next group therapy session."

That had to be a significant offer, but I didn't know what to say beyond, "Thanks."

God, she was beautiful, never more than when she was vulnerable, her light brown eyes wide open, as wide as her heart.

"But JD, I'm just not ready. I'm never getting back with you until I know it's forever. I can't break up with you again." She folded her arms across her pretty flowered dress and hugged herself as she turned away, surprising me more than if she'd slapped me. She gripped her upper arms until they turned white under her fingers. "I wasn't ready in college, either. I thought I was ready for anything, between my parents and the nuns and, okay, that man, the one I never told you about."

"You don't have to," I interjected, feeling sick.

Ignoring me, she plowed ahead. "My best friend's father. He grabbed me in the changing room by his swimming pool and put his hands everywhere. I shoved him and got away, ran home in my swimsuit. He hit his head on the concrete and suffered a concussion. Didn't suffer nearly enough, I thought, but the family almost lost their house because he was out of work so long. It wasn't my fault!"

"It wasn't your fault!" I chorused at the same time. Our minds work together. I wanted to hold her, but she radiated a fence, if not a thick stone wall.

"So I went to college thinking nobody was going to take anything from me, that I'd share myself with whomever I wanted, now that nobody could tell me what to do. And the first week of classes, I met you."

The silence went on long enough for my heart to drop to the basement and down to earth's core. I'd viewed our first days together differently, often with the word *magic*.

She shook her head, her dark wavy hair flying everywhere, a chaos I adore. "I wasn't ready, not for love. So of course it didn't work out."

"That time or the next time or the next." Each one was like a knife.

"And now I'm still not ready. I had my life all planned by the time I set foot on campus. I got the degrees I intended, the jobs I said I wanted —and then I quit and came here. I said I wanted to live alone, to never be responsible for or accountable to anyone again."

"Yes," I whispered. "Exactly."

"I never wanted a garden because it was just a chance to get me and my clothes dirty, more work I didn't need. I didn't want pets because they're a lot of work. And now my career is on a runaway wagon, careening to who knows where, but not to the big firm partnership of my dreams."

She sounded so confused. At least I always knew I didn't want the judgeship or corporate partnership of my family's dreams.

"Now I live in a madhouse with half an acre of vegetables and flower beds and my very own cat. Not even a smart cat, so I'm always cleaning up after her. But I love her. And I love you and everybody I live with, and I can't believe how much I love it all, even Darryl's holiday decorations. But I don't know who I am anymore, and it's sinking in that I never did. So how can I commit this person I don't know to anybody else? Only, then I think you're bound to marry someone—"

"Not Heather. Promise."

"That makes me feel better."

I stepped closer and touched her shoulder from behind. "I love it here too. And you, in whatever form you'll accept. Let me know if you ever want to discover who we are together. It's possible I could be up for that."

She turned back to me and held out her arms. "I will. But for now, just dance me to—"

"The end of love?" I asked, quoting my favorite Leonard Cohen song title as I put one hand on her back and traced down her arm with my fingers until I held her hand like a dove. The heavy gardenia scent came near to overpowering me.

Blinking her eyes at hummingbird speed, she smiled at last. "That's not off the table, but I meant dinner."

I sang Mr. Cohen's languorous tango in her ear and drew her body against mine in a way that would have gotten us arrested in the last century, the only way to have her close for now. I led her down the dance line of our gallery-hallway, in turns, weaves, and dips, back into our present life.

Dance me to the end of love.

# CHAPTER 30
# JD: FRIDAY NIGHT, BEAUCHAMP

Dinner aromas enveloped us halfway down the hall, making my stomach growl. I recognized fresh-baked bread and Mexican spices; the rest was a mélange that I'd have to separate to identify. After one last twirl and a long, deep lunge, Dianne dove into the kitchen chaos. Me, I'd have chosen to run, but someone would expect me to do something for the meal. Only fair, if I wanted to eat it.

Suddenly I understood Johnny's turning this meal into a religious ritual. I don't know the original meaning of Shabbat, but everyone here was doing something for somebody else for higher reasons. For Cherry's favorite food, Dianne's sisters and cousins wrangled tamales and enchiladas, trying to imitate their grandmother's recipes. Chantal argued with them over the right way to make cornbread. Johnny's grandmother oversaw the black-eyed peas, Merry's choice, and the kugel, without which no special occasion could be worthy of that name. Its light cinnamon scent wafted toward me like incense. Johnny pulled the challah bread pans out of the oven, clanging them onto the cooling racks. The smallest pan held a wheatless loaf for Chantal. Chantal, ready to sing prayers for someone else's religion, now poured glasses of wine while Darryl poured the grape juice. I waved to him and pointed to the grape juice for me.

Good grief, even my father was helping, instead of glowering from a corner, as he was wont to do. He and Zap were adding three leaves to the already long dinner table.

Still the big sister in charge, Dianne plowed through, checking on dishes and consulting with Johnny.

Both Merry and Cherry leaned against the backdoor, eyeing the confusion. Merry asked, "How do you ever get a meal prepared?"

"We have a system," I said as Dianne handed me the bucket-sized salad bowl full of vegetables, which reminded me of Passing the Peace in church. Maybe it wasn't necessary for me to touch her warm hand in the process, but she smiled, so it was okay. "And her name is Dianne. Do you two want to help? We can go out onto the back porch away from the havoc."

Dianne glanced toward the front door. "People are arriving. Cherry, could you greet them? If they bring food, they can put it on the buffet table. I'll have JD's father and Zap set that up next. We're going to have too much to put it all on the dinner table at once."

I collected cutting boards, knives, and peelers for Merry and me, and we set up operations on the back porch table. The temperature grudgingly inched down to near-bearable, making the wind not so hot, though the copse of trees on the side of the house protected us from its full blast.

"So how's school?" I asked, bracing myself for the worst as I mangled a tomato into smaller parts. Johnny taught me how to slice and dice in college, but I've never managed to do it longer than five minutes, not even that long tonight because I was hungry. The tangy aroma made my stomach growl again.

She smiled as she tore lettuce into bits. Good thing Johnny couldn't see. "Bearable. Funny how after the Thompson lawyers stormed the administration, they decided that I could retake last spring's finals and either do my courses remotely or test out of them. The ... jerks didn't come back. I don't know whether that's due to your efforts, their being charged with attempting to murder Johnny, all the other girls coming forward and their rape kits being tested, or what, but it makes it easier to walk around campus. So thank you, bro, for everything."

"I mostly tagged along with the grownup attorneys and snarled on cue. Those guys are good. I'm glad I'll never go up against them in court, what with Grandfather being retired and Dad's corporate practice never intersecting with what I do." I whacked a cucumber into small pieces, releasing the sweetish scent I never knew it had.

"That's so funny when Granddad is such a pussy cat."

"He is?" I tried to imagine that label applying to U.S. Attorney James David Thompson, (retired) (a.k.a. Granddad).

"Totally! He's going to enclose their dining room to make a nursery, and Granny can hardly wait. Dad? Well, I'm sure by the time the kid's thirty, he'll stop saying that it's not too late to consider adoption. I'm thinking no."

Merry seemed to have walked her way into a decision to have and keep the baby. I couldn't imagine making her choice, even with all the brands of therapy she'd had. But her eyes shone clear and confident. A deep calm practically hummed through her.

The backdoor slammed as Cherry joined us. "Johnny says to chop this stuff up for the salad. Who puts squash in salad?"

"People who planted a quarter acre of it," I said.

As she took the bowl from her sister, Merry said, "We should be fine, staying at Granny's. Grad school funding starts next September. And listen! Dad's promised to increase Cherry's and my allowances and keep them going until we're twenty-six, and then taper them off until we're thirty. I'll be able to do grad school at a leisurely pace, maybe even take an internship."

Cherry yawned. "You're welcome. I told Dad that you and I were coming back home after college. I don't know which he thought was worse: nightly theater parties until dawn or a screeching rug rat."

"That must be why he's talking about selling the house again and moving into a one-bedroom condo," I said. "I'm glad he's extending your allowances, with Cherry aiming to replace Meryl Streep and Merry with the baby and grad school. By the way, how long do I keep calling this new human 'the baby?' High school graduation?"

Merry gave me that secret smile that used to mean trouble. "The doctor thinks she's a girl, though it's a few weeks before we can tell for sure."

"And maybe years before she tells us," added Cherry.

Merry continued, "If so, her name is Jade Adrienne Arline Thompson. I'm calling her Jadey."

Cherry poked me with a claw-length nail, red with stars. "Get it? In reverse order, that's Thompson for Dad, because forget that guy. Then Arline for Granny, Adrienne for Mommy and me, and finally Jay-Dee. See?"

Merry beamed. "For the best brother ever."

Cherry shook her head. "What is with this family that they keep inflicting family names on their innocent children? Fair warning, I'm naming my kids Axolotl and World Peace."

I turned away, trying to dislodge something in my throat. Through the window into the kitchen, I could see everyone at their preparations. Without sound, they looked like they were conducting an elaborate church service.

I knew I was being the standard emotionally stunted Thompson male. I wished Santa would bring our family an emotional Rosetta stone this next Christmas. Until then, I'd have to stumble along on my own.

While I tried to make my tongue say real words, Darryl popped out of the house, waving his camera. "Smile, guys. I'll make you all stars, at least on Black Orchid social media."

Swell. Another Thompson children photo, this time with the background of challah, cornbread, kugel, and tamale aromas instead of Easter candy.

"You sure are a happy bunch," Darryl said as he clicked away. "I'm putting this up on Family Friday for certain."

Later it had the honor of going up on my office wall: me and my sisters, arms around each other, grinning for sheer joy.

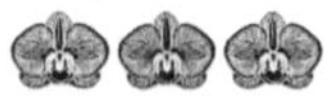

Want to know what JD and friends do next? Sign up for Beauchamp News at https://dimond.me for the latest news, a free story about the Black Orchids' college days, and more.

# PLAYLIST

While reviewing *Family Matters* at your favorite bookseller, enjoy the playlist, all the songs the Black Orchids listened to or sang in this adventure:

https://spoti.fi/3OFjfyN

1. Samba de mon coeur qui bat, Coralie Clement
2. Reina del Baile, ABBA
3. Chiquitita, ABBA
4. Margaritaville, Jimmy Buffet
5. Margarita, Traveling Wilburys
6. Tequila Makes Her Clothes Fall Off, Joe Nichols
7. Besos De Fuego, Ricky Martin
8. Mama Mia, ABBA
9. Al Andar, ABBA
10. Gracias Por La Musica, ABBA
11. Ring Ring, ABBA
12. No Hay A Quien Culpar, ABBA
13. Mi Gente, J Balvin, Willy William
14. Tu Sonrisa, Elvis Crespo
15. Kizomba Love, Afro Connexion

16. Oye Como Va, Santana
17. Corazón Espinado, Santana, feat. Mana
18. Dance Me to the End of Love, Leonard Cohen

Watch JD and Dianne's tango at
https://youtu.be/VAq8mHYWafY.

# ABOUT THE AUTHOR

After stints in professional orchestras, law firms, cat rescue, bookkeeping, and technical communication, M. R. Dimond returned to a childhood dream of writing fiction, which has turned out to be about musicians, lawyers, veterinarians, accountants, and cats.

Sign up for the newsletter to learn the next Black Orchid Enterprises mystery, or see some previous works:

- *Birth of the Black Orchids,* Black Orchid Enterprises Mystery Book 1
- *The Sphynx Who Stole Christmas,* Black Orchid Enterprises Mystery Book 2
- "Playing It Again" in *Hook, Line, and Sinker,* Seventh Guppy Anthology, edited by Emily P. W. Murphy
- "Be It Resolved" in *Riddles, Resolutions, and Revenge,* R. B. Marshall, collator
- "Blessed" in *Dreaming the Goddess,* Karen Dales, editor
- "Nine Lives Through Time" in *Cat Tails, War Zone,* Rebecca McFarland Kyle and Dana Bell, editors
- "Carol for Mixed Voices" in *Best of Strange Horizons Year 2*

Find me on Facebook as Madeleine.Dimond and Instagram as MRDimondAuthor.

# PREVIEW OF HALLOW,
# BOOK 4

"It's beginning to look a lot like Sukkot, every-where you go," I sang, kidnapping an old Christmas favorite. "There's a sukkah on your front porch, where you can eat your borscht, along with many people you don't know."

As I returned to my office in Gregg House's southern ground-floor turret, my three-time ex, current business partner, and permanent friend Dianne Cortez (CPA, CFE)

danced into her office in the northern turret across the gallery hall. She spoke in a percussive chant as accompaniment to my song. "Halloween is coming, coming, just you wait, just you wait. I long for the good old holidays in corporate land, corporate land. A rope of dull tinsel and a half-hour party is good enough, it's good enough for me."

We live and work with another college housemate (Johnny Ly, DVM) in a Victorian mansion that somehow plopped down in Beauchamp, Texas, twenty-two miles from Austin and many more from anywhere else. Two turrets jut out in front, where Dianne and I have our respective offices. The semicircular windows gave us a great view into the tent-like sukkah, attached to the front porch, and of the lawn, where the entire population of Beauchamp and beyond tramped across to take the advice of the yard sign: "Eat your lunch in the sukkah!"

It was, of course, our intern's idea and execution. Darryl Swann assists Johnny in the cat hospital, Dianne with never-ending tax returns, and me with my legal grind. Decorating for the holidays, all the holidays, brings Darryl enough joy to keep him doing those other jobs, so it's worth it.

And he brings in business, more than any of our floundering marketing efforts. Ever since the Passover-Easter-Oestara debacle, about which we do not speak—though you might have seen it on TV—word would spread around Beauchamp like chiggers in the grass when Darryl put up a new display. People suddenly remembered their cats' vaccinations, burning tax and accounting questions, and even legal matters, such as divorce. But I'm sure that couple would have split up anyway.

Darryl's current cunning plan involved an extravaganza for the Jewish High Holy Days—all of them—to bribe Johnny into allowing a haunted house in the front yard for Halloween. Johnny hated Halloween.

But Darryl's vision of Sukkot involved attaching a three-sided hut, or sukkah, to the front porch. I had doubts that clients would make their way through it. They'd have to push through Darryl or Johnny giving Sukkot workshops for young and old and then brush aside the curtain of dangling squash and corn decorations, all before they reached the front door.

I was wrong, at least in one case.

On the third day of Sukkot Darryl brought in one middle-aged couple, saying, "JD Thompson—Mr. and Mrs. Abreu. I gotta get back to the lulav-making craft before the kids go feral."

The newcomers didn't look old enough to be my parents, though success can shave off many years. As we seated ourselves in my office, I touched my great-grandfather's nameplate for luck, like I always do. He was the first James Thompson, attorney at law.

My visitors cast approving glances around the Victorian mansion and antique furnishings of dark old wood and red velvet. I didn't mention that I was renting from Johnny's grandmother.

A young tabby cat jumped out of hiding and skittered across my desk.

The dark-haired woman laughed. "Can I pet her?"

"She lives for it," I said as I handed over the little purr-slut.

The sandy-haired man gave his wife an affectionate smile as she cooed and stroked the cat snuggling in her lap. "Judge Pereira said you weren't the average lawyer."

That surprised me, his former clerk. "Probably true. Is that what you want?"

"Perhaps. Families can get stuck in their own ruts. We read about your sukkah on a mailing list. I wanted to get legal advice about my father's will and a family mystery. I liked the idea of consulting someone Jewish. It's good to see another blond, blue-eyed Jew," said Mr. Abreu with a laugh.

"Methodist, actually," I said, tapping my phone to summon Johnny. "My partner Johnny is Jewish and in charge of mysteries. I'm happy to help with the legal side."

Mr. and Mrs. Abreu looked at the top of the bookcase next to my desk, where a large, twisted ram's horn lay.

"Since I played trombone in high school, Johnny thought I should play the shofar for High Holy Days," I explained.

"Did you blow it every day during the previous month and then one hundred times on Rosh Hashanah?" asked Mrs. Abreu.

My lips twitched in painful memory. "I did. It moved Johnny to tears, but that was because it reminded him of a dying rhino he tended in his zoo vet residency. So I can't say I got the music out of the shofar, just suffering."

A ghost of a smile flitted across the man's face. "Music isn't the point."

His wife nodded with an affectionate look in his direction.

"That's what Johnny said."

Johnny came down the gallery-hall at that moment, escorting his latest vet patient and client. Usually his clients go in and out the house's north side door, directly into the clinic.

"Kiera wants to see the—what is it?" asked a woman's voice over a cat yowling in its carrier.

"Sukkah," said Johnny. "For the Feast of Tabernacles. Our intern Darryl and I are conducting a workshop. I'm going out now to explain the religious elements."

"Can I stay, Mommy? Can I?" demanded a young voice. "You can take Snowball home and come back and get me."

Johnny went outside with them and appeared at my door a few minutes later. I made explanations and introductions, with the couple insisting on being Vidal and Miri, now that we knew each other better.

As Johnny lowered himself in one of the channel-stitched chairs, he said with precision, "In one sense, yes, I am Jewish. My grandmother is Jewish, but my mother is not. I am converting."

Both Abreus nodded in approval. Vidal pulled out the thinnest attaché case I'd ever seen, close to a file folder, and then pulled out a document, also thin.

That was cute. I couldn't remember the last time anyone handed me papers. That's why on the eighth day God invented the Cloud. As I skimmed the will and probate papers, Darryl's voice carried through the open windows. "And you tie the three branches together to make your lulav, kind of a plant-based light saber. Then you wave it around in six directions. That doesn't mean find six people to hit!"

As the lightsabers rustled and whacked, they filled the air with sharp, woody fragrance.

Johnny's brows drew together. "I hope that's not disrespectful."

"The rabbis are always trying to reach the younger audiences, so maybe not." Miri shrugged. "But if you want the advice of an experienced teacher, use cardboard, pool noodles, and nerf balls, not real branches and fruit."

"I think you're right." Johnny had to raise his voice over the commotion outside as the young ones chased each other with their new weapons. "Not five minutes after I said the prayer with them and they're already at war."

That summed up everything we needed to know about both religion and war. I continued with my part of the job. "I'll look at it harder and calculate the separate and community property, but offhand I don't see anything unusual. It looks like one-third of the estate went to the widow, with a life interest in the real property, and two-thirds divided between his four children, one of those children being from a previous marriage."

"That would be me," said Vidal. "Please look at the phrase after the children's names."

"'...so long as they embrace our heritage.'" I frowned. "That phrase has no legal definition. Even if the rest of the family is more religious—"

Miri sniffed. "His eldest half-brother's wife calls it kosher when she puts the bacon on a separate shelf in the refrigerator."

"—the estate is already distributed," I finished. "The court isn't likely to reverse that."

"You don't know my brothers!"

"Half brothers," emphasized his wife. "His father's new wife and her sons did everything possible to push him out of the family."

Vidal protested, "As a child, I was happy to be pushed out. My mother's best friend, my Auntie Rose, always opened her door to me. I never doubted my place in my father's heart. His growing up in the shadow of the Holocaust meant he'd never be like the fathers on TV. But he split his estate evenly between us, very fair."

"Wills are the septic tanks of families," I observed. "No matter how great or small the inheritance. Why would your brothers challenge the will now?"

"They've never stopped!" exclaimed Miri. "Since the day his father died, they've complained. They tried to claim Vidal exercised undue influence on his father in his last days."

I flipped through the papers again, checking the dates. "Must have been a hard case to prove, with the will written ten years before and the even distribution of the assets. If I were going to unduly influence someone, I'd make sure I got the whole enchilada, not equal shares with my siblings."

"It was ridiculous. Everyone saw that. Everything they've tried is ridiculous. One of them claimed he wanted to live in the house he'd grown up in."

Miri sniffed. "As though his wife would consent to live in a 1950s ticky-tacky house with one bathroom."

"I said, of course, he could have the house and give the each of the rest of us a quarter share of the current market value. That would be fair." Vidal's voice grew heavy. "That wasn't what he had in mind. I should just give him my share out of brotherly love."

"And it was all a scam, because his wife told me they intended to sell it as soon as they got the title."

"Your other brothers wouldn't like that," I observed.

"They were in on it! They were going to get part of the purchase price, not as much, because they wouldn't have fixed up the house for sale, but they didn't mind sharing with each other, only me." Vidal's sigh sank down to our basement level. "When I think how important family was to my father, because he'd lost all his, and my brothers and I can't even carry on a civil conversation."

"That's hardly your fault," said Miri, patting his arm.

They exchanged a look while the kids outside pelted each other with etrogs. The part of etrogs being played by fat lemons in our celebration, a sharp citrusy aroma soon filled the room.

Vidal continued in a heavy voice. "Kids, right? My daughter thought it would be fun to get a DNA test. She gets the results, and then an email through the company, obviously a form letter sent to multiple people." He handed me another paper.

Hello,

Your DNA test identifies you as a relative of my husband Mitchell Wade. He died serving his country. He never knew his blood relatives and was estranged from his adoptive family. I wanted as many relatives as possible to know him, even at a distance, so his memory doesn't die with me.

I said, "Given that the letter writer doesn't ask for contact, on a generous day, I would say thank you, express my sympathy, and write his name in the family Bible if I had one. What relation is he to your daughter?"

"Her father," said her father.

Silence fell like velvet, except for the screams of the lulav lightsaber brigade outdoors.

I shut the windows and inhaled the last of the crepe myrtle scent. "That must have been a shock for you."

"Not half as much as for me," said the girl's mother.

Join the newsletter at https://dimond.me/ to learn when *Hallow* is available and receive a free short story